Praise for *The Green Eagle Score*

"Donald E. Westlake (who writes as Richard Stark when he wants to see how far he can push it) has a wonderfully twisted mind that takes impish delight in knocking over its own elaborate plot constructions."

Marilyn Stasio, *New York Times Book Review*

"Richard Stark's Parker . . . is refreshingly amoral, a thief who always gets away with the swag."

Stephen King, *Entertainment Weekly*

"The Parker novels . . . are among the greatest hard-boiled writing of all time."

Financial Times

"You can read the entire series and not once have to invest in a bookmark."

Luc Sante

"Stark . . . is a mystery connoisseur's delight. . . . A tremendously skillful, smart writer."

Time Out New York

"It's excellent to have [Stark's novels] readily available again—not so much masterpieces of genre, just masterpieces, period."

Richard Rayner, *L. A. Times*

"The caper novel, the story of a major criminal operation from the point of view of the participants, has no better practitioner than Richard Stark."

Anthony Boucher, *New York Times Book Review*

"Westlake's ability to construct an action story filled with unforeseen twists and quadruple-crosses is unparalleled."

San Francisco Chronicle

"The Parker books meditate with surprising profundity on human desire and attachment at their fantastic extremes."

Leonard Cassuto

"Richard Stark's Parker novels, a cluster of which were written in an extraordinary burst of creativity in the early '60s, are among the most poised and polished fictions of their time and, in fact, of any time."

John Banville, *Bookforum*

"Gritty and chillingly noir . . . [Westlake] succeeds in demonstrating his total mastery of crime fiction."

Booklist

"No one can turn a phrase like Westlake."

Detroit News and Free Press

"Elmore Leonard wouldn't write what he does if Stark hadn't been there before. And Quentin Tarantino wouldn't write what he does without Leonard. . . . Old master that he is, Stark does them all one better."

L.A. Times

The Green Eagle Score

Parker Novels By Richard Stark

The Hunter (Payback)

The Man with the Getaway Face

The Outfit

The Mourner

The Score

The Jugger

The Seventh

The Handle

The Rare Coin Score

The Green Eagle Score

The Black Ice Score

Deadly Edge

Slayground

Plunder Squad

Butcher's Moon

Comeback

Backflash

Flashfire

Firebreak

Ask the Parrot

Dirty Money

The Green Eagle Score

RICHARD STARK

With a New Foreword by Dennis Lehane

The University of Chicago Press

The University of Chicago Press, Chicago, 60637

University of Chicago Press edition 2010

Printed in the United States of America

19 18 17 16 15 14 13 12 11 10 2 3 4 5

ISBN-13: 978-0-226-77108-3 (paper)
ISBN-10: 0-226-77108-3 (paper

Stark, Richard, 1933–2008.
The green eagle score : a Parker novel / Richard Stark ; with a new foreword by Dennis Lehane.
p. cm.
Summary: Parker plans to steal the payroll from a U.S. military base.
ISBN-13: 978-0-226-77108-3 (pbk. : alk. paper)
ISBN-10: 0-226-77108-3 (pbk. : alk. paper) 1. Parker (Fictitious character)—Fiction. 2. Criminals—Fiction. I. Lehane, Dennis. II. Title.
PS3573.E9G7 2010
813'.54—dc22

2009039267

♾ The paper used in this publication meets the minimum requirements of the American National Standard for Information Sciences—Permanence of Paper for Printed Library Materials, ANSI Z39.48-1992.

Foreword

I had drinks with Donald Westlake once at a crime fiction conference in the winter of 2000. We talked mostly about two terrific scripts he wrote in the late eighties, one for Stephen Frears (*The Grifters*), the other for Joseph Ruben (*The Stepfather*), but we never discussed his alter ego Richard Stark or Stark's indelible creation, Parker. This would be less surprising if I weren't such a geek about the Parker books. I'd read them all in the summer of '86, (there were sixteen at that point.) Along with Elmore Leonard's work, they taught me nearly everything I know about how to execute violence on the page. As for Parker himself, he's a watershed character in American noir, nearly incomparable. So why didn't I fly my geek flag while hanging with the man who created him?

A sense of mystery, for one; I don't want to know too much about the artists who create the art that excites me. The collective dream that descends upon the reader of a fictional universe depends on believing that the dream is quite real, even while you know, of course, that it's not. I feared the more I learned about the mechanical strings behind Parker the more artificial he would seem. And finally, the writer is about the last person you should trust when it comes to interpreting his work. If we truly knew what we were doing, we probably wouldn't do it; it would feel too much like a straight job.

As to Westlake, himself, he matched my preconceived impression of the creator of the John Dortmunder novels—a wry, intelligent man, self-deprecating and steeped in irony.

Such was Donald Westlake. Richard Stark, however, was nowhere to be found. Because as playful as Donald Westlake is, Richard Stark is all business. Where Westlake's writing is chummy, Stark's is clinical. If Westlake is the guy you'd love to find sitting beside you at the bar on a raw March night, Stark is the guy you'd hope to avoid in the parking lot on your way home.

As a stylist, Richard Stark's sense of economy is surgical. He has no time for flatulent prose; one senses he holds the decorous in contempt. He evokes a world of medium-sized, nondescript cities or dusty flatlands. A lot of the action takes place in motel rooms, either the kind with wrought iron fire escapes right out the window or those "with concrete block walls painted green, the imitation Danish modern furniture, the rough beige carpeting, not enough towels." Like those motel rooms and like Parker, Stark is a model of efficiency. This isn't to say his style lacks amenities. The swift sentences move with a running back's fluid timing. He could no more be accused of soulless functionality than could Hemingway or Raymond Carver. Stark writes with economy, yes, and cold, cold clarity, but there's grace in the prose, a stripped-bare poetry made all the more admirable for its lack of self-consciousness.

And what did that cold clarity produce?

Parker. The greatest antihero in American noir. If Parker ever had a heart, he left it behind in a drawer one morning and never came back for it. He never cracks a joke, inquires about someone's health or family, feels regret or shame or even rage. And not once in the sixteen novels that comprise the FPE (First Parker Epoch, 1962–74) does he wink at the reader. You know the Wink. It's what the "supposedly" amoral character does to let the reader know he's not *really* as bad as he seems. Maybe, in fact, he's been the good guy all along.

Parker *is* as bad as he seems. If a baby carriage rolled in front of him during a heist, he'd kick it out of his way. If an innocent woman were caught helplessly in gangster cross-fire, Parker would slip past her, happy she was drawing the bullets away from him. If you hit him, he'd hit you back twice as hard. If you stole from him, he'd burn your house—or corporation—to the ground to get his money back. And if, as in *Butcher's Moon*, the sixteenth of the sixteen FPE novels, you were stupid enough to kidnap one of his guys and hold him hostage in a safe house, he would kill every single one of you. He'd shoot you through a door, shoot you in the face, shoot you in the back and step over your body before it stopped twitching.

Nothing personal, by the way. He gets no pleasure from the shooting or the twitching. He's not a psychopath, after all, he's a sociopath. But first and foremost, he is a professional. He's the progenitor of many a fictional criminal antihero, but those progeny are always redeemed by a need to connect with the human race. James Ellroy's antiheroes come immediately to mind, and it's hard to think of a more resolutely scumbag act than the protagonist of *White Jazz* throwing a mentally handicapped man out a window in chapter one. Yet by chapter thirty, he's reached out to the reader along the lines of shared humanity, and he's garnered our empathy, if not our love. Similarly, in the films of Michael Mann, many of the protagonists, from Frank in *Thief* to Dillinger in *Public Enemies*, share Parker's emotional retardation and consummate professionalism, but in that very professionalism Mann finds nobility. Cop Vincent Hanna in *Heat* clearly admires the work ethic of criminal Neil McCauley, while Frank in *Thief* asks the cops who shake him down why they don't try, as he does, to actually work for a living. But in the moral universe of the Parker novels, the very idea of nobility is laughable—Parker *is* a sociopath. The world he inhabits, however, is worse.

It's a world of absolute rot. Nothing and no one is above it and most are happiest that way. The Outfit sits atop a pyramid comprised of luckless thugs, idiot muscle, hustlers, grifters, hookers with hearts of bile, and bloody avarice so banal yet so all-encompassing as to wallpaper every room in every scene of every one of the sixteen Parker novels. The Outfit casts its shadows everywhere. It's the grimy engine that runs the grimy car with the faulty brakes and the crap transmission, yet when the brakes blow and the transmission seizes, the Outfit tells you it's your fault. And your bill.

Who can fight against this? Not the hero with the heart of gold. Not the Nice Guy or the Good Guy or the Morally Compromised But Ultimately Nice Good Guy. No. Only a cog in the machine can screw up the machine. A piece of the machine as grimy and hard as the rest of it. A chunk of steel. Or pipe of lead.

Parker is the lead pipe. He has no illusions about the machine—not a single ideal left to shred or a romantic notion left to dispel. Like the machine, he is heartless. And this is where he differs from every other antihero in noir. James Ellroy's protagonists have heart, however deeply buried. Jim Thompson's characters might not have heart or sentimental notions, but they are ultimately punished for that lack. Same goes for James M. Cain's lecherous ids-run-amok. Hammett gave us Sam Spade, he of the physical resemblance to the devil, who finds his partner's killer not out of noble principle but solely because it would be bad business not to. But while Spade may have no feelings for Archer, he is in love with Brigid O'Shaughnessy. Again, humanity creeps in whether the protagonist wants it to or not. This is a foundation brick of literary narrative—the antihero discovers his humanity, which allows us, the readers, to recognize ourselves in him and feel communion with the human race as a whole.

To which Parker says, screw that. Parker refuses to reveal his heart. Parker authentically and resolutely eschews sentiment. Or emotion. Parker never asks for understanding or grasps for a common cord between himself and the reader. (If the common cord held monetary value, he'd steal it. Otherwise, it's all yours.) What Parker represents, at least to me, is the abolition of the wish fulfillment that forms the firmament of narrative literature, a firmament I, myself, usually require, both as a reader and a writer. The wishes being fulfilled are familiar—good wins out, love conquers all, crime never pays, the check is in the mail. Well, in this case, the check *was* in the mail, but Parker intercepted it. And cashed it. And used it to finance a crime that paid double what you'll make this year.

So why do we like him for it? Why do we root for him? Why is it, after reading sixteen novels depicting the adventures of a heartless sociopath in the summer of '86, did I feel the desire for more? Why do I still look back on these novels, as a reader, with great affection and, as a writer, with wonder?

I still don't know the answer. Not absolutely. I *suspect.* I suspect we all recognize the Lie, even as we wrap our arms around it and hug it tight to keep us warm. The Lie is the illusion that we are safe, that we are watched over, that we will go gently and that the night is good. Not so, says Richard Stark. Not so, says Parker.

We are not safe. No one is looking out for us. And the night? The night is dark. So let's get to work before the sun comes up. Before someone catches us at it. Before the world wakes up.

Dennis Lehane

The Green Eagle Score

PART ONE

1

PARKER LOOKED in at the beach and there was a guy in a black suit standing there, surrounded by all the bodies in bathing-suits. He was standing near Parker's gear, not facing anywhere in particular, and he looked like a rip in the picture. The hotel loomed up behind him, white and windowed, the Puerto Rican sun beat down, the sea foamed white on the beach, and he stood there like a homesick mortician.

Parker knew him. His name was Fusco.

Parker rolled over and called to Claire, a wave away, "I'm going in."

"Why?" But then she looked toward the beach, and didn't need an answer. She paddled over near Parker and said, "My God, he's inconspicuous. Who is he?"

"Business, maybe. You can stick around down here." He knew she wouldn't want to hear about business.

"I'll work on my tan," she said. "Will you come back?"

"Yes. Don't get too much sun."

He let the long waves glide him in toward the beach, and when he waded out onto the sand Fusco was gone. He walked up to his chaise longue, toweled himself dry, slipped into his sandals, draped the towel around his shoulders, and crossed the sand to the rear entrance of the hotel. He was a big man, blocky, with a big frame and an efficient graceless way of moving.

It took him a second to adjust to the darkness inside the door. He stood on the carpet until he could see, then walked down the long corridor to the hotel lobby. As he crossed the lobby Fusco got up from one of the black leather chairs and strolled obliquely across Parker's route and into the cocktail lounge. Parker went on to the elevator, rode up to seven and went down the hall to his room. The air conditioning was on and the room was as cold as a piece of tile. Parker called room service, ordered tonic and ice, and got dressed. Then he stood at the window, looking down at the tourists walking along Ashford Avenue, until the knock sounded at his door.

It was the tonic and ice. He signed for it, got a glass from the bathroom and the gin from the dresser, and made himself a drink.

The glass was half-empty before Fusco arrived. Parker opened to his knock and Fusco came in saying, "Christ, it gets hot down here."

"That's what it's for." Parker shut the door. "Make yourself a drink."

"What's that, gin? I can't touch it." Fusco shook his head and patted his stomach. "It's a funny thing," he said. "Since I got out I can't touch the hard stuff, it makes me double right up."

There was nothing to say to that. Parker went over to the chair by the window and sat down.

Fusco said, "Maybe some ice water. Okay?"

"Go ahead."

Fusco was medium height and very thin. His face was lined as though he worried a lot. Parker hadn't seen him in ten years, but he didn't seem to have aged at all. Having been inside had affected his stomach, and maybe was making him act so hesitant, but it hadn't been bad for his appearance.

Parker waited while Fusco built himself a glass of ice water, and then he said, "You could of tried looking like a tourist."

Fusco frowned like a man worried about constipation, his forehead laddering, and said, "Christ, Parker, not me. I put them Bermuda shorts on, hang a camera around my neck, I look like a pickpocket headed for Aqueduct. I got to stay who I am."

Parker shrugged. "Anyway, you're here."

"I got the address from Handy."

That was unnecessary to have said; Handy McKay was the only one Parker had given the address to. Parker had some of his drink and waited.

Fusco said. "I don't like letters through the mails, you know? And telephone calls when it's a complicated thing like this. So I figured I'd come down myself, personally, tell you about it."

Parker sat there and waited to be told.

Fusco looked worried again. "Handy said you were looking for work. I wouldn't of come down otherwise."

Fusco had to have some kind of reassurance, or he'd never get to the point. Parker said, "I'm available."

Fusco flashed a brief nervous smile of relief. "That's good," he said. "I'm glad." But then he didn't say anthing more.

Parker prodded a little, saying, "You've got something on?"

"Right. You remember that wife I had? Ellen?"

Parker vaguely remembered hearing that Fusco had married, but it had been only five or six years ago, long since Parker's last meeting with him. But it was simpler to nod and say, "Yeah, I remember."

"I don't know if you ever met her—"

"I didn't."

"Yeah, I didn't think so. Anyway, she divorced me when I got sent up. A little over three years ago. You know I got a daughter?"

Parker shook his head, not giving a damn. "I didn't know that," he said.

"Three years old," Fusco said. "Four in July."

Afraid Fusco was going to come out with baby pictures in a minute, Parker said, "What's this got to do with the job?"

"I'm getting to it," Fusco promised. "Ellen, now, after she divorced me she went back home to Monequois, that's a little town in upstate New York, near the border. You know, the Canada border."

Parker nodded, holding his impatience in check. The only thing to do with these run-off-at-the-mouth people was wait them out, they'd get it all said sooner or later. Try to rush them and they'd just get derailed and leave out half the things you should know.

"She lived with her folks for a while," Fusco said, "but I guess they gave her a bad time. About me, or something. So she went off on her own and got a job at a bar outside of town there. See, there's this Air Force base there, it's huge, and across the road from the gate there's all these bars, you know?"

Parker nodded.

Fusco said, "After a while she started shacking up with one of the guys from the base. Stan Devers, his name is. What the hell, I don't blame her. She's divorced in the first place, and I'm in stir, so why not?"

Where was all this leading? Parker couldn't see a job anywhere in the story yet, and it was spreading out wider and wider all the time, getting more and more soap opera. Parker said, "What's the point of all this?"

"I'll tell you in a minute," Fusco said. "You got to understand the background, is all."

Parker shrugged. "All right, Let's hear the background."

"The main thing," Fusco said, "is this guy Stan Devers. He's just a kid, you know, maybe twenty-three, twenty-four. Younger than Ellen, you know? But he's okay. When I first got out, and went up to see Ellen and the kid, and there's all these uniforms and things in the closet, I got mad, you know? Naturally. Also I was a little short, I didn't have nothing stashed away when I took the rap. So I tried to lean a little on this Devers kid, and he was a real surprise. He's a sharp kid, he knows his way around. He's never been in on anything like our stuff, you know, but he's cool."

"You couldn't badger-game him, you mean."

Fusco shrugged, not seeing any humor in it. "It was worth a try," he said, "but with Stan it wouldn't work out. But we got to know each other, you know? Sit around, have a Coke or whatever, throw a little bull. He's a good kid."

Parker said, "So now you're buddies. And he's got an idea for a heist."

"It was my idea," Fusco said. "He wasn't sure at first but I talked him into it and now he's a hundred per cent. And I know what you're thinking about amateurs, but not in this case. Stan's as good as half the pros in the business."

Parker said, "Half the pros in the business are in the big house."

"You'll have to see the kid for yourself," Fusco said. "If you don't think you can work with him, naturally you don't stick around. But like I told him, what we need is an organizer. Neither of us could set this thing up right, and I don't ever again go into a job that isn't set up right. That's what happened the last time, and it isn't going to happen again. I told Stan I'd try to get you, I told him you were the best blueprinter in the business. He's the one sprang me for me flying down here, a hundred twenty bucks. He's a good kid, and he's serious, and this thing can work."

Parker said, "Why do you need him?"

"He's the inside on the thing," Fusco explained earnestly. "He's a clerk in the base finance office, and—"

"Wait a second. The base finance office?"

Talking fast, Fusco said, "Parker, they got five thousand men on that base, they pay twice a month, they pay cash, the whole thing's—"

Parker broke in, saying, "Wait a while. This is the job you came down here to offer me? Go steal an army payroll right off the post?"

"It isn't Army, Parker, it's Air Force. And besides, they—"

"What do you mean it isn't Army? Have they got a fence around the post?"

"Base, they call it a base."

"Have they got a fence around it? And gates? And armed sentries on the gates?"

"Parker, it can be *done*. There's better than four hundred grand in there, Parker, twice a month, ours for the taking."

"Yours for the taking," Parker told him. "I don't take money away from five thousand armed men."

"It isn't five thousand armed men, Parker. Christ, you

know what Stan calls the Air Force? The saluting civil service, he says. You know what they carry on their practice alerts? Empty carbines. They don't even get bullets, for Christ's sake."

"Somebody's got bullets," Parker told him. "Somewhere on that post, base, whatever they call it, somewhere there's somebody doesn't want us to take that four hundred grand. I'll leave that somebody alone."

"Parker, we got an *inside* man!"

"That's right. So if we do go in, and we do get back out again with the cash, who's the first guy the law talks to? Your pal."

"I told you," Fusco said urgently, "Stan's okay. He'd carry it off, Parker, I know he would."

"You don't know anything about him," Parker said, "until he's gone through it. That's what the word amateur is for. It means somebody you don't know about because he hasn't gone through it before and you can't tell what a guy's going to do until he's done it once."

Fusco spread his hands. "Parker, what can I say? I'm convinced."

Parker looked at him. Fusco was convinced, all right, but what did it mean? Was it the pro in him that was convinced, or was he locked into the kind of desperation that hits a lot of men, even the good solid pros, when they first make the street after a stretch on the inside? Lack of money has something to do with it, because most men fresh from stir have spent whatever they used to have on lawyers, but there's also the need they feel to get back on the horse, to prove to themselves they can still operate, the fall they took was nothing but a fluke, a one-in-a-million shot that can't possibly happen again. So they get impatient and they take the first thing that comes their way and they wind up back inside.

But Parker wasn't impatient. He had a stake, and reserves stashed here and there, and no need to prove anything to himself, and he could wait till the right thing came along. His reserve fund wasn't deep enough to satisfy him, particularly with Claire along now, and that's why he was looking for work, but the search had in it no overtones of urgency.

Claire was responsible for a lot of the absence of urgency. For the last few years before her, he'd been finding himself moving more and more in the direction of work-for-work's sake, work to relieve the boredom of being alive and not involved in a job, and that was a habit of mind just as dangerous as the ex-con's desperation. It was on a job that he'd taken in spite of knowing it was bad, a job set up like this one of Fusco's by a recent ex-con and an amateur inside man, that he'd met Claire. The job had gone sour in a lot of different ways, but at least out of it he'd gotten her, and calmness, and the ability to look at this thing Fusco was offering him, and decide whether or not it was something he wanted to get involved in.

Parker finished his drink, got to his feet, walked over to where the ice and gin were on the dresser, and made himself another. When he sat down again he said, "Tell me about your inside man."

"A kid," Fusco said. "Maybe twenty-four. College boy. Got kicked out of ROTC for some reason, that's why he's an enlisted man. Works in the finance office, clerk there."

"He's got keys?"

"Sure. He isn't supposed to, you know, but he got himself a set."

"Who knows he has them?"

"Me and Ellen. Now you."

Parker shook his head. "What about his buddies on the base?"

"He ain't that kind," said Fusco. "He's a loner, Parker. He's got a couple buddies he drinks with sometimes, but he wouldn't tell them nothing."

"You sure? Maybe he wants them in on it."

"Hell, no." Fusco was very emphatic. "Parker, I tell you the kid's sharp, he knows you get professionals to do a professional job. He already told me, the string we put together doesn't look good we can forget it, he's out."

Parker said, "What about when the law leans on him afterward? They will, you know."

"He'll keep his head."

"How do you know?"

Fusco made vague hand movements. "Because I know the kid. You'll know it yourself, when you see him."

"It doesn't necessarily kill the job if we have to do it the other way," Parker reminded him.

Fusco was too far inside his own ideas to get what Parker meant. He said, "What other way?"

"If we have to lose the kid when the job's over."

"You mean, bump him?" Fusco seemed really shocked. "Christ, Parker, I told you he's okay."

"Any record?"

"I don't think so. He's only a kid."

"Kids can have records."

"You'll have to ask him, I don't know."

Parker shrugged, said, "All right, let it go. What about this ex-woman of yours?"

"Ellen? What about her?"

"She's in on it, isn't she?"

"Sure," said Fusco, throwing it away, as though he didn't know why Parker would bring it up at all. "She knows about it, if that's what you mean."

"Does she sit in, or just kibitz?"

"Oh, no," Fusco said, "Ellen wouldn't want to work. But it's okay her knowing. What the hell, she used to be with me, she knew all about everything I worked. She's reliable, guaranteed."

"What's the set-up between you and her?"

Fusco shook his head. "Nothing," he said. "Ellen don't want me back, so that's the way it is. She's seeing some headshrinker, she's got it all doped out, we shouldn't of got married in the first place, it's nobody's fault, nobody should get mad at nobody."

"And between you and Devers?"

"I got no jealousy, Parker. You know me better than that."

"That's you. How does he act, you, the ex-husband, hanging around?"

Fusco shrugged. "He's cool. What the hell, he knows the

score, he knows I'm not trying to freeze him out."

"All right. Tell me about this base. You say it's Air Force."

"Yeah." Fusco leaned forward, elbows on knees, expression earnest and intent. "It's some kind of training base, it's all schools. They get a big turnover of people, most of them only stay two or three months."

"What kind of planes do they have there?"

Fusco seemed surprised at the question. "I don't know," he said. "You want to go in by plane?"

"How do I know? I'm not sure I want to go in at all. Do you know anything about this base or don't you?"

"Stan would be the one to tell you about that," Fusco said. "I don't know this military stuff, Parker."

"You never cased it?"

"Sure I did." Fusco's professional pride was hurt. "I been on the base a couple times, Stan fixed me up with a fake ID."

"How far's the finance office from the gate?"

"Well, there's three gates. It's a hell of a distance from the main gate, but there's this other one, the South Gate, it's only like two blocks from there. It's like a back entrance."

"How many guards on each gate?"

"Two. Just kids, you know?"

"And the payroll's four hundred grand?"

"Around that. Sometimes a little more, a little less."

"How's it come in?"

"They fly it in, the day before."

Parker said, "Give me the sequence."

Fusco said, "The plane comes in the day before, in the morning. The payroll's in two metal boxes. They put it on this truck, drive it to the finance office. Then they—"

"What kind of truck?"

"Regular armored car. A tough nut, Parker."

"All right. What next?"

"They split it up," Fusco said, "into the payrolls for all the outfits on the base. The money and a payroll sheet goes into a small metal box for each outfit, and it all goes into their vault overnight. Then in the morning they load it all into the armored car again and drive it around the base.

There's one officer in each outfit takes care of the payroll. He signs for his box, takes it, gives out the cash."

"What's the overnight surveillance?"

"Two AP's inside the building, in the room next to the vault."

"AP's?"

"Air Police."

"How many people work in the finance office during the day?"

"I don't know for sure. Maybe twenty. That's the kind of thing Stan could tell you."

"Maybe he should of come down here."

Fusco grinned. "Would you listen to a kid you didn't know?"

"I'm not sure I'll listen to you either," Parker told him. "What do you want from me now?"

"Come back with me. Talk to Stan, look it over, make up your mind. If you don't like it, Stan pays your round trip. And the lady's, if you want."

Parker emptied his glass again, got to his feet. "I'll let you know," he said, and went over to the dresser to get out his other bathing-suit. While changing he said, "You registered here?"

"No. I'm at the Holiday Inn out by the airport."

"What room?"

"Forty-nine."

Wearing the bathing-suit, Parker went into the bathroom for a dry towel. When he came out he said, "You go back there, I'll get in touch with you."

"It's solid, Parker," Fusco said. "I'm sure of this one."

"Take your time with the ice water," Parker told him. "Make sure the door's locked on your way out."

2

CLAIRE WAS lying face up on her chaise longue, arms at her sides, eyes closed, one knee raised. Her suit was yellow and two-piece, her skin was tanning nicely, her face was made anonymously beautiful by her sunglasses, and the men watching her looked at Parker with disgust when he sat down beside her and said, "I'm back."

She opened one eye, nodded, and closed it again. "He's a funny-looking little man."

"His ideas are funny too."

"Don't tell me," she said, and her body seemed to have tensed slightly, without actually moving.

"I won't tell you," Parker said. Claire's one involvement in a heist had been too much for her, and now they had a deal; she would never ask him what he was working on, and he would never volunteer to tell her. It was a perfect arrangement for both of them.

She said, after a minute, "Are you going away?"

"I don't know yet." He put his towel down beside him on the chaise longue and said, "I'm going in and get wet."

"I've had enough for a while. I'll stay in the sun."

He walked down across the sloping hot sand to the water. Two tanned women in white bathing-suits, coming out together, pulling off their bathing-caps and shaking out blonde hair, looked at Parker through their lashes, trying to upstage one another, but he ignored them both. There was a time when women had been a brief antidote for the itch to work, but now that he had Claire the quick anonymous lay was no longer necessary. He walked on past them and into the water, and when it was thigh-deep he stretched forward into a breaking wave, rode the trough and up the face of the next one, and rolled over to coast with the motion of the sea.

He kept one eye on the beach, not wanting to lose his orientation. The ocean here could turn bad all at once, and he wanted always to know where land was. Just yesterday a young couple had been caught in some kind of backwash, the waves refusing to ride them in but instead keeping them imprisoned out there, slowly pulling them away until they'd had to call for help, and fresher swimmers had gone out after them and towed them in to where they could stand. Parker respected the sea, as he respected any powerful opponent, and was in no hurry to challenge it.

Was he going to join Fusco in challenging the United States Air Force? On the face of it it didn't seem sensible, but every job seemed impossible before it was done. This one was being presented to him by a professional he'd known for years, so even though Fusco was recently out of prison Parker had to think about his proposition, he couldn't dismiss it out of hand.

And maybe Fusco really did have something. He was still a pro, with a pro's eye and a pro's judgement, so maybe up there in upstate New York with the ex-wife and the payroll clerk and the United States Air Force there was a workable job to be done after all.

And if it could be, if the details could be found, the right string put together, all the dangers thought of and defended against, if they really could walk into that Air Force base and walk out with the payroll, what a sweet one that would be.

It wouldn't cost anything to take a look. If it didn't feel right he didn't have to stay. Claire would be here, he could come back, rest again, relax again, wait again for somebody to come along with an offer that sounded better.

All right. He rolled over, drifted lazily in to shore, walked up the beach in the sunlight to where Claire was lying now on her stomach, propped up on her elbows as she read a paperback book.

Parker sat down beside her, put his sunglasses on, leaned back on his chaise longue with his face in the sun, and said,

"I'm going away for a while."

Still looking at the book, she said, "I knew."

"It may just be for a day or two. If I'm not back in two days figure me to be gone for a couple weeks at least."

"Or maybe for ever," she said.

He looked at her, but her eyes were still on the book. He said, "I'm not walking out on you."

"Maybe not on purpose," she said. "I've known men like you before."

She might have been talking about her airline pilot husband, who wound up smeared like raspberry jam across some mountaintop. Parker didn't like the analogy.

"You've never known anybody like me before," he said. "I only walk where the ice is thick."

"You walk on ice," she said. "That's what I mean."

"That's a surprise? You knew that all along."

"I know."

"Then why this?"

She turned her head, looked at him through the green lenses of her glasses. After a minute she shook her head and looked back at the book. "I don't know. No reason."

"All right." He faced front again and said, "The room'll be paid for a month. If I'm not back by then, there's a package in the hotel safe, enough to carry you for a while."

"If you're not back in a month, I shouldn't wait any more, is that it?"

"Right."

"You won't be contacting me at all."

"Probably not. I might, if there's a reason, but I won't just to say hello the weather's fine."

"I know," she said.

Parker got to his feet. "Don't get too much sun."

"I'll be going in in a while," she said.

Parker took his towel and walked across the sand to the hotel. He looked back when he reached the door, but Claire wasn't looking at him. Her head was down on the book now, and her hands were covering her face. Parker went on into the hotel.

3

"STAN," SAID Fusco, "this is the fella I told you about. Parker, Stan Devers."

It was raining in New York, drizzling down on the airport in the darkness, cold and wet and a million miles from the heat of Puerto Rico. People with intent faces were hurrying by, bumping into each other, carrying luggage, in a hurry, not happy. In the middle of the brightly lighted floor Parker and Fusco and Devers made an island that the bustle eddied around, the hurriers managing to miss them without quite seeing them.

Devers stuck out his hand. "I've heard a lot about you, Mr Parker." He was a pretty beach boy, muscular and smiling and self-confident, with a clean strong jawline and curly blond hair. His handshake was self-consciously firm, and he was in civilian clothing, in threads a little too good for somebody who's supposed to be living on Army pay. He made Parker think of the kind of insurance salesman who peddles his policies on the golf course, except this specimen wasn't quite old enough for that yet.

"I've got a car outside," Devers said.

Fusco had explained to him on the way up that the fastest way to get to Monequois from New York was to drive. There was local airline service, but it was slow and unreliable. That's why Devers had been contacted to drive down and meet them at Kennedy Airport.

They started now toward the exit, Devers leading the way through the crowd, saying over his shoulder, "It's about a five-hour drive, so if you want to make any kind of stop now, go right ahead."

"We'll stop on the way," Parker said.

"Fine."

The doors opened for them and they went out to moist cold air. There was a roof over this area, but everything was wet just the same, glistening with a clammy sheen of moisture. A Carey bus was picking up passengers to the left, and a stream of taxis was inching along the ramp, letting out arriving passengers and picking up new ones.

Devers had illegally parked his car, a two-year-old maroon Pontiac, in a loading zone just to the right. He unlocked the trunk and stowed the luggage while the others got into the car. Fusco started to get in front but Parker stopped him, saying, "Sit in back. I want to talk to your boy."

"Sure thing."

Devers showed surprise for just a second when he got into the car and saw Parker in the front seat with him, but all he said was, "The longest stretch'll be getting out of this damn city." He started the engine, cut off a taxi, and they rolled down the ramp into the rain.

Devers was a good driver, if a little fast and cocksure. He out-distanced most of the cabs he met while circling around Kennedy Airport and out on to Van Wyck Expressway, and from there on he maintained a steady seven or eight miles above the posted speed limit. It was just a little after midnight now, and traffic was pretty light once they moved away from the airport. Devers stayed on good roads all the way, Grand Central Parkway and the Triborough Bridge and then over to the Major Deegan Expressway, and despite the rain they were only about half an hour getting to the beginning of the Thruway at the New York City line.

Parker waited until then, until Devers was on the Thruway and settled in for the straight run north, the tires whining on the wet concrete, the wipers ticking back and forth, and then he said, "What are your payments on a car like this?"

Devers was surprised at the question. He looked at Parker, seemed about to ask him why he wanted to know, but then shrugged and looked back at the highway and said, "I don't know exactly. I paid cash."

Parker nodded, and looked out the window, and when a minute later Devers asked him if he minded a little music he said no. Devers found a rock-and-roll station, but he kept the volume down and the tone control toward bass, so it wasn't bad. Most of the time, the beat of the music worked against the pace of the windshield wipers.

They stopped at the Ramapo service area near Sloatsburg. Sitting in a booth over a late dinner, Parker said, "That's a good-looking suit you've got."

Devers smiled in pleasure, glancing down at himself. "You like it?"

"Where'd you get it? Not in Monequois."

"Hell, no. Lord & Taylor, in New York." Devers spoke like a man justifiably proud of his store.

Parker nodded and said, "You go there much?"

"I got a charge account there," Devers told him. "Lord & Taylor and Macy's, between the two I can get anything I want."

"I guess so," said Parker, and went back to his meal.

When they went out to the car, the rain had stopped. The Pontiac glittered in the lights from the restaurant, looking almost black. This time Parker had Fusco get in front while he sat in back. Devers glided them back out to the almost-deserted Thruway, took it up a little above seventy, and turned on the radio again. It was a different station now, but it was playing the same music.

Nobody talked. The dashboard lights were green, the night outside the windows was rarely punctured by headlights. From time to time Parker saw Devers looking at him in the rearview mirror; the boy kept studying him, with curiosity and respect and some puzzlement.

Parker shut his eyes and listened to the night whine by under the tires.

4

COLD BRIGHT sunlight flooded in when Parker opened the door. He gestured and Fusco came in, saying, "You had breakfast?"

"Yes." Parker shut the light out again and said, "Sit down."

It was a room in a motel in a town called Malone, about fifteen or twenty miles from Monequois. It was a standard small-town motel, with the concrete block walls painted green, the imitation Danish modern furniture, the tough beige carpeting, not enough towels. Parker had learned years ago that you don't take up residence in the place where you're going to make your hit, so this would be home for him either until the job was over or until he decided he wanted to bow out of it. Fusco was already staying in Monequois, had been for the last few months since he'd gotten out, so there was nothing to be done about that, but he and Devers had let Parker off here last night on the way in, arranging for Fusco to borrow the Pontiac and come back for him this morning.

Now, sitting down in the room's only chair, Fusco said, "You want to talk about Stan."

"He's either very good or very bad," Parker said. "I want to know which one it is."

"He's good Parker. What makes you think he's anything else?"

"How long's he been tapping the till?"

Fusco looked blank. "Tapping the till?"

"Come on," Parker said. "He's got himself an angle going in that finance office, he's bleeding off a couple hundred a month, maybe more."

"Parker, he never said a word to me, honest to God."

"Would he have to tell you?" Parker asked him. "He goes to New York to buy a suit at Lord & Taylor, on his charge account. How much you think that suit set him back?"

Fusco spread his hands. "It never even occurred to me. I don't think that way, Parker, I take a man at his word."

"You used his car to come here just now?"

Fusco frowned, rubbed a knuckle across his jawline. "That's a pretty good car, isn't it? I never thought about it. You think he's been hooking the company, huh?"

"He didn't tell you about it," Parker said. "That's good. Buying the car with full cash down was stupid, but if he keeps his mouth shut maybe he's all right anyway. How well do you get along with this ex-wife of yours, what's her name?"

"Ellen. She still calls herself Ellen Fusco."

"You get along with her?"

"Sure, why not?"

"Well enough to ask her a question about Devers?"

Fusco shook his head. "I'm not sure, Parker, that's the honest to God truth. What kind of question?"

"I want to know did he ever tell her what he's got going."

"You want to know how he works it?"

Parker shook is head in impatience. "I want to know if he opened his mouth to her."

"Oh." Fusco nodded, saying, "Sure. I can find out something like that. Not directly, you know what I mean?"

"Any way you want to do it." Parker lit a cigarette, walked over to drop the match in the ashtray on the nightstand. Looking at Fusco again, he said, "Back in San Juan, I said the job could be done maybe even if Devers wasn't solid. You didn't like that."

"Because he is solid, I know he is."

"I don't know it," Parker told him. He waited a second, and said, "How important is Devers to you?"

"Important?" Fusco looked confused. "What do you mean, important?"

"I mean, what if Devers looks like a problem to me? What

if I say the job is good but Devers is bad? What if I say we run it and bump Devers? Do we go ahead, or do we forget the job?"

Fusco spread his hands, for just a second at a loss for words. Then he said, "Parker, the question won't come up, I know it won't."

"I'm bringing it up now."

Fusco shook his head, looked at his outspread hands, looked over at the window where sunlight made bright slits across the venetian blind. Finally, not looking at Parker, he said, "What it is, I'll tell you what the problem is. It's Ellen, it's — I don't want Ellen to — I wouldn't want her to think it's because of her. That I rigged the whole thing to bump Stan because of her. That's what she'd think."

"What does it matter what she thinks?"

Fusco shrugged, kept looking away toward the window. "She'd want to get even, get back at me. She'd blow the whistle."

"You mean they'd both be unreliable." Parker flicked ashes into the ashtray. Watching Fusco, he said, "We could handle her the same way."

Now Fusco did look at Parker, surprised and shocked. "For Christ's sake, Parker! She's got my kid, I told you that! For Christ's sake, you can't — you don't just—"

Parker nodded and walked toward the door. "That's what I wanted to know," he said. "What the rules are."

Fusco was still sputtering. "Parker, we're not going to—"

"I know we're not. But I have to know the limitations. Now I know. Devers has to be all right, or the job's no good."

Fusco looked at him.

Parker shook his head. "I don't want to kill your kid's mother," he said. "I want to know what we can do and what we can't do, what kills the job and what keeps it alive." He opened the door, and sunlight sliced in. "Let's go."

"You scared the crap out of me," Fusco said. He got to his feet, grinning weakly. "The next thing I thought you'd say, I thought you'd say, okay, we'll bump the kid, too."

"I didn't think you'd go for it," Parker told him.

5

"ELLEN," SAID Fusco, "this is Parker. Parker, my ex-wife."

Ellen Fusco said, "How are you?"

Parker nodded. "Good."

Ellen Fusco was something different from what he'd expected. A short intense bony girl, she would have been good-looking except for the vertical frown lines gouged deep into her forehead and the way she had of looking at the world as though challenging it to a spitting contest. She looked as though she should go through life with her hands always on her hips.

Her home reflected this attitude of belligerence. It was shabby, but clean, as though neither fancy frills nor dirt would ever dare enter here. The furniture was usual enough, from the swaybacked sofa to the table-model televison set on its wheeled stand, but the bookcase was maybe a little larger than in the average living-room, and the books it contained were for the most part fairly heavy reading, Sartre and de Beauvoir, the James brothers, Uwe Johnson, Edmund Wilson.

Her clothing showed the same truculent plainness. She was wearing black slacks, a short-sleeved gray pullover sweater, brown loafers, no socks. Her hair was black and long and straight, held together with a rubber band at the nape of her neck. She wore no makeup or nail polish, as though the image she was trying to get across lay somewhere between a Greenwich Village bohemian and a Nebraskan farm wife.

Fusco said to her, "Is Stan up yet?"

"He's in the bathroom."

Parker looked at his watch. Ten-forty.

Ellen Fusco said, "You want some coffee?"

"Sure thing," said Fusco. "What about you, Parker?" He was somewhat eager, somewhat nervous, and couldn't make up his mind whether he should play host or not. He'd been married to this woman, he'd brought Parker here to her house, but there was another man in the bathroom.

"Black," Parker said, talking directly to Ellen.

"Make yourselves comfortable," she said, and went through the arched doorway into a small crammed white-and-yellow kitchen. This kitchen opened directly from the living-room, so she could be seen moving around in there, getting the coffee ready.

As Parker sat down in the armchair near the door, Fusco said, looking around, "I guess Pam's out in the back yard. That's my kid."

He looked around at Parker, seemed about to say something more, and then to realize this was neither the time or the place — nor was Parker the man — to ask him if he wanted to go out in the backyard and take a look at a three-year-old girl. Fusco turned away, moved vaguely in the direction of the kitchen, or maybe just toward the back window there, but then abruptly turned back and sat down in the middle of the sofa. They sat in silence then, Fusco fidgeting slightly and looking this way and that, Parker unmoving, waiting.

Ellen's coming in from the kitchen with the coffee was simultaneous with Devers' arrival through the other doorway, dressed in fatigue trousers and T-shirt. He was barefoot and looked still half-asleep. He saw the coffee and said, "One of those for me?"

"Get your own," she said.

Devers stood with a pained smile on his face, trying to find something to say, while she put the two coffees on tables handy to Parker and Fusco. She didn't look directly at anybody while doing this, and left the living-room right away, going out the door Devers had come in.

Devers beamed his painful smile at Parker and said, "Domestic bliss. It's just a funny game we have." But when Parker just looked at him without saying anything, Devers shrugged and got rid of the embarrassed smile and went over to sit on the sofa beside Fusco. He picked up Fusco's coffee cup, drank some, made a face, and said, "You know I like it with sugar." He put the cup down, looked at Parker, and said, "You want to see the base today, right?"

"That's right."

"We'll take a run out there. You mind if I make myself some breakfast first?"

Parker shrugged. "We're in no hurry. I want to know some things first anyway."

"Name it."

"How long have you been stationed here?"

"Eleven months."

"Finance office the whole time?"

"Right."

"You RA or US?"

Devers frowned. "What's that?"

"Maybe they changed things," Parker said. "It used to be, RA on your serial number meant you enlisted, US meant you were drafted."

"Oh. That's Army. There's no draftees in the Air Force."

Fusco said, "You enlisted?" He couldn't believe it.

Devers grinned at him. "I'm no place getting shot at, am I?"

"What's your term?" Parker asked him.

"Four years."

"How much to go?"

"Seven months. I did a year in the Aleutians before I came here."

Parker said, "You want to hold this job up till you get out?"

"That'd be smart. I leave the office, then they get held up. They'd come looking for me."

Parker nodded. He knew that was true, but he hadn't known whether Devers would understand it or not. He said, "What about the way it is now? Only seven months to go."

"There's two short-timers in the office," Devers said. "One's getting out in three weeks, the other one in two months."

"So the law will look at them before they look at you."

"That's what I figure."

Parker said, "But they will look at you."

Devers nodded. "I figured that, too."

"How long've you been working your dodge in the office?"

"What dodge?"

"The dodge you bought the Pontiac with."

Devers grinned and shook his head. "I saved my money while I was in the Aleutians."

"You got bank records to prove it?"

"Do I need them?"

"Yes."

"I didn't keep it in the bank."

"Where did you keep it?"

Devers was getting irritated despite himself, the smile was slipping slowly from his face. "What's the point?" he said. "We're talking about robbery, not embezzlement."

"The law," Parker told him. "They'll check out everybody in your office. They'll say, 'There's a kid with charge accounts in New York, expensive clothes, expensive car. How'd he do all that on Air Force pay?' Then they look very closely at you, just to see what happens."

Devers bit a knuckle, frowning, thinking. Finally he said, more as though it were a question than a statement, "I had my grandmother hold it?"

"Your grandmother? Why?"

"I always got along with her best," Devers said. "My mother and father split up, I wouldn't trust my mother with the prize from a Cracker Jack box. So I gave my money to my grandmother, and when I got back to the ZI she gave it back to me."

Fusco said, "Back to the what?"

"The States," Devers told him. "ZI. Zone of Interior."

"Christ," said Fusco.

Parker said, "Your grandmother's going to cover for you?"

Devers grinned. "Guaranteed. She died in April."
Parker said, "What if they check with your mother?"
"What my mother says is her business. She'd say something different from me just out of spite."
"Would she?"
Devers hesitated. "Who am I talking to now? Parker or the law?"
"Does it matter?"
"No. No, you're right. I've told you the straight story."
Parker said, "You got a checking account?"
"Sure."
"Let me see the checkbook."
"Oh." Devers nodded. "Yeah, I see what you mean."
Fusco said, "What's the problem?"
"My deposits," Devers said. "Like, I put in a hundred thirty last week, so where did it come from?"
Parker said, "Where did it come from?"
"Give me a minute," Devers said.
Parker waited, but when Devers kept on concentrating he said, "You're a sitting duck, Devers. You aren't covered at all. They could land on you any time."
"They've never had any reason to look me over."
Parker said, "What if somebody else in the office tries something, and he's clumsy? So they find out there's something wrong, they start looking around, and you stick out like the Empire State Building."
"God damn it." Devers gnawed his cheek. "There's got to be some way to cover."
"Not the old lucky at cards routine," Parker told him. "That way, you've got to get half a dozen other people to say yeah, they played cards with you, they lost to you. That's too many people."
"I know. I wouldn't try that one anyway. Let me think about it while I make some breakfast."
Parker finished his coffee. "All right, we'll be back at twelve."
"Fine."
Parker got to his feet, and Fusco bounced up after him.

They went out to the sunlight and got into Devers' Pontiac. Fusco said, "Which way?"

"Gas station. We want gas and a roadmap."

"Right."

As they drove, Fusco said, "You were right about him. I mean, hitting the company."

"The question is," said Parker, "can he work out a cover."

"He's a smart boy, Parker."

"Maybe."

They came to a gas station and Fusco pulled to a stop beside the pumps. While the attendant pumped gas, Fusco went into the office and got a map. He brought it out and handed it to Parker, already folded to the area around Monequois.

They were in an out-of-the-way northern corner of New York State, close to the Canadian border, about fifteen miles west of Malone, north of Route 11. The nearest city of any size was called Massena, farther west, large enough to have a commercial airport. The border was about twelve miles to the north. Dannemora, the New York State penitentiary, was about forty miles to the east.

Fusco paid for the gas whle Parker looked at the map. They drove out of the station and Parker said, "Let's go north, toward the border."

Fusco looked at him in surprise. "We won't want to go crossing any borders, Parker."

"I know that. But they'll figure us to try, so let's see what the road looks like."

Fusco shrugged and went back to driving.

Monequois was a small town, overbalanced by the Air Force base just outside the town limits. There were more people on the base than in the town, so the influence showed up everywhere, in the names of bars and diners and motels, in the heavy preponderance of blue uniforms on the downtown streets, in the number of bars and movie houses. If the majority of people at the base had been permanent rather than transient, the effect on the town would have been even greater, but as it was the place was unmistakably a camp town.

They had to go through town and out past the air base to Route 95. It was scrub country out here, hilly but not mountainous, heavily forested. Very little of the base could be seen from the road, only a few drab slant-roofed buildings glimpsed through the trees and then the sudden complex busy structure of the main gate, like a stage set in the sunlight, with a dark blue billboard on one side giving, in gold letters, the names of the military organizations here, all done in incomprehensible abbreviations.

Fusco turned north on 95, went up to Bombay and took the unnumbered road up to Fort Covington. This was a smaller and less traveled road than to continue on to Massena or to take the bridge across the St Lawrence from Rooseveltown to Cornwall on the Canadian side.

They went through Fort Covington, but stopped on the other side before reaching the border. Parker said, "All right, let's go back."

It didn't look good. No place had shown itself readily as a hideout. The forest was thick between the little towns, but it wasn't empty. Most of the woods were posted against hunters, and the rest would be full of them. It didn't look likely for them to come up here after the job and cool out somewhere short of the border.

Of course, he couldn't be sure yet, and anyway this was doing it backwards. If Devers couldn't cover his embezzlements there wouldn't be a job anyway. And even if he could, there was still the base to be looked at. The whole thing might be impossible because of some element long before the getaway or hideout.

On the way back, Fusco said, "What if he can't do it?"

"Like you said before," Parker told him. "If Devers isn't solid, the job's off."

Fusco frowned. Parker could feel him pushing for Devers to come up with something.

6

ELLEN OPENED the door again, gave them a sour look. "You two." She stepped out of the way.

Parker and Fusco went inside. As Ellen was shutting the door, Parker said to her, "What's the problem?"

Not looking at him, turning away, being busy about something else, she said, "Problem? No problem at all." She walked away across the living room.

Devers, sitting at the kitchen table with the remains of a pancake breakfast in front of him, waved his fork and called, "Be right with you."

Parker ignored him, saying after Ellen, "Is it just Devers? What's on your mind?"

She kept moving away, and Fusco, in the manner of somebody embarrassed and trying to avoid a scene, said quickly, "Parker, let it go."

"No." Parker pointed at Ellen and said, "Stop right there. I want to know what's stuck in your craw."

Ellen turned around, at the far end of the room, moved her chin in a contemptuous nod toward Fusco, and said, "Let him tell you." But she didn't leave the room.

Parker looked at Fusco, who shrugged and said, "She's just a little bugged, Parker, that's all. It don't mean a thing, it's just the way she gets."

"About the job?"

Fusco looked scared. "Parker, I swear to God she's no problem. She always takes the dim view, that's all it is."

"She was this way before?"

"That's why she left me," Fusco said, "the time I took

the fall. Because that time she was right."

Ellen's lip curled, but she didn't say anything.

Devers had walked in from the kitchen, carrying a coffee cup in his hand. "And now she's sore," he said, "because this time her ex-husband's got me involved in it. Gonna get me in trouble." Standing there, he drank coffee, with Ellen glaring at him.

Parker said, "What will she do about it?"

Ellen answered him. "Nothing," she said, biting the word off. "You don't have to worry about me."

"That's straight, Parker," Fusco said.

Parker looked at them, Fusco scared, Devers confident, Ellen angry. He considered, and finally shrugged, letting it go. For now he'd take their word for it, and just keep his eyes open. Over the years he'd come to accept the fact that the people involved in every heist were never as solid as you wanted them. They always had hang-ups one way or another, always had personal problems or quirks from their private lives that they couldn't keep from intruding into the job they were supposed to be doing. The only way to handle it was to watch them, know what the problems were, be ready for them to start screwing up. If he sat around and waited for the perfect string, cold and solid and professional, he'd never get anything done.

"All right," he said. "She's your woman."

Grinning, Devers said, "Which of us you talking to?"

Shocked, Fusco said, "Stan!"

Ellen said to Parker, "You finished with me now? Can I get back to what I was doing?"

"I'm finished," Parker told her.

"Thanks."

She left the room, and Parker turned to Devers. "What about that checking account?"

The way Devers was smiling, he'd thought of something. He said, "You know the song about the little tin box?"

"No. What's the idea?"

"I didn't want to put all my cash in the bank," Devers said. "All I'd do was put in enough money to cover my checks and keep a small steady balance. But most of my money I keep in a box in the closet in the bedroom here."

Parker said, "Why?"

Devers grinned and shrugged his shoulders, being boyish and innocent. "I don't know, it's just the way I've always done it. I guess I'm like King Midas or something. I like to have my money where I can look at it. You have to have a checking account these days, you can't send bills through the mail and money orders are too much trouble, so what the heck I've got an account. But the money isn't real to me if it's in the bank. I like to be able to open my box and *see* the money there."

Fusco was frowning at Devers as though he couldn't understand what the boy was up to, but Parker could see it. It was the kind of offbeat approach to money a kid might have. If Devers could pull it off.

Parker said, "Let's see this little tin box."

Devers held up a hand. "Give me time," he said. "I'll have it when it's needed."

"You going to go buy a new box?"

"Hell, no. I'm going to have the little old box I've carried with me ever since high school, the battered old box that went with me to Texas, to New Mexico, to the Aleutians, and now here. Don't you worry, Mr Parker, that box is going to look *right*."

"Not overdone."

"You mean, decals from the different places?" Devers laughed. "I can be subtle, Mr Parker," he said.

Parker said, "How much you got left in this little box?"

Devers frowned. "I'm not sure. Not much, after all the stuff I bought. It depends when we do it. If it's the next payroll, that's next Tuesday—"

"Too soon."

"Fine. Then I'll have maybe six, seven hundred."

"You've got the math worked out? So they can add up your income and your outgo and it'll work?"

"Oh, sure. I could go up to twelve hundred and still be within the possible." Devers grinned and said, "But I like to leave a little slack, it adds that touch of credibility."

"Give me a list of people at these different places," Parker said, "that saw the box."

Devers looked startled, but recovered quickly, saying, "Nobody. I didn't let anybody know I had it."

"Why not?"

"Here and there in the Air Force, Mr Parker, you run into a thief."

Parker considered, and then nodded. "All right," he said. "It should cover. If you can run it right."

"I can run it," Devers said.

"With a cop leaning on you?"

"Cops have leaned on me before," Devers said.

"For something this big?"

"No. But I can do it."

The worst thing about the boy was his confidence. He was smart, he was fast, he was capable, but he knew he was all those things and that could hurt. But he'd been running his dodge at the finance office almost a year without being caught out, so maybe his confidence wouldn't be a liability. Parker was now willing to take a chance.

He said, "Answer me one question. Straight."

Devers spread his hands. "If I can."

"You've got a nice thing going at this finance office. It seems safe and sure and profitable. This knockover's got to be risky. Why not stick with what you've got?"

"First," Devers said, "I've only got seven more months of this gravy train. If I re-enlist I'm bound to get transferred out pretty soon, probably overseas again. Besides, I'm not all that happy with Air Force life. So when I get out, where am I? I've got a car, some clothes, a few hundred in cash, and a nice way to cut the pot in an Air Force finance office. Big deal. I go to work someplace else, maybe in a bank or something, and it takes me a while to figure an angle. Maybe they're tougher than the Air Force, in fact they probably are, so maybe I don't figure an angle at all. The point is, what I've got is fine for right now, but what about the future?"

"What will you do with your chunk?"

"Live on it," Devers said. "Not loud, but comfortable."

"And when it's gone?"

Shrugging, Devers said, "I'll worry about that when the time comes. What this does, it buys me a year or two. Then I'm where I would have been when I got out anyway."

Parker knew he was looking at a new recruit to the profession, knew he was aware of it before Devers. Devers had been tapping the Air Force for money for this month, next month, the month after that. Now he was coming into the heavy racket to take care of this year, and next year he'd be coming back, looking up Parker or Fusco or whoever else might be getting into this string, saying, "You need a boy any time, I'm available."

If things went well this time. Devers hadn't been tried yet, not one hundred per cent. He could still blow, he could still fail to have the nerve for it. But Parker thought the odds were with the boy.

"All right," he said. "You were going to show me the base."

"Right," said Devers, "Hold on, I'll get your ID."

7

THIS WAS the bad moment, walking up the blacktop toward the gate. Devers went first, a little ahead of Parker and Fusco. They were all in their normal civilian clothing, which Devers had told them would cause no comment. "Most guys are in civvies any time they're off duty," he'd said. He'd also explained that because the base was full of technical schools, which ran on shifts, it wasn't unusual to see men off-duty at any time of the day or night.

They were coming to the main gate rather than the one nearer the finance office because here the traffic was heaviest and they were the least likely to get any kind of close study. Parker in particular had an ID card with a picture far from his own appearance, though the relationship between Fusco's face and that on his card was also slight. "They won't look," Devers had said. "You just open your wallet and wave it at them as you go by." He'd demonstrated, holding his wallet open at arm's length.

Parker had thought they would go in Devers' car, but the boy had been against it. "We'll be noticed," he said. "There's a bus out from town, it's always full of guys. We take that, get off with them, everybody goes through the gate in a bunch." So they'd driven downtown, parked the Pontiac a block away, and boarded the civilian-operated bus out to the air base. It was about half-full, and as Devers had said, most of the passengers were in civilian clothes.

Now they'd reached the base. The three of them were in the middle of the straggling group of twenty-five or so walking up to the gate in the sunlight. The two APs stayed inside their shack, looking through the window at the IDs held up for their inspection, nodding, their expressions bored.

You could only go by the shack in single file. Devers went first, Fusco second, Parker third. Parker noticed that most of the men ahead of him barely glanced at the APs on their way by, so he did the same. Their bored expressions didn't change as they looked at his card, and a second later he was inside, putting his wallet away.

"We'll take the bus," Devers said. "This is a damn big base, the office is way to hell and gone over there."

"There's a special bus just for inside the base?"

"Sure. Run by the Air Force. Actually there's three routes, but they all come by here. We want a number one."

"They run all night?"

"Yeah." Devers looked at him. "You thinking of something?"

"I'm just asking questions," Parker told him.

It was true. He didn't know whether a bus would work into this heist any more than he'd known whether or not they'd use a plane when Fusco had asked him about it back in San Juan. He wanted to know about transport, vehicles everything that moved and traveled and had reasonable justification for being on this base. What he could use and what not he'd find out later on.

The first bus that came they didn't want, but most of the others waiting with them did. As they all climbed aboard, Devers said, "That's the bus goes to the transient barracks area. Those are all our scholars."

"What kind of schools?"

Devers shrugged. "Everything. Everything from Personnel Technician to A & E mechanic."

"Translate both of those."

"Okay," Devers said, grinning. "A Personnel Technician is a clerk typist in the orderly room. A & E is aircraft and engine. A greasemonkey."

"What about military police? Do they have a school here?"

Devers looked surprised, and said, "Be damned! That's one they missed."

"Good."

Fusco said, "Here comes our bus."

The bus was dark blue and rickety, with the engine in front, like a truck. The driver was wearing fatigues, with Airman First Class stripes on his sleeve. There were only about ten people in the bus, scattered here and there. Parker sat by a window on the right side, about halfway along. Devers sat beside him and Fusco slid into the next seat back and leaned forward to listen.

Devers gave them a running commentary as they went along, pointing out the PX, the mess hall, the NCO club, building after building. They were all similar, as though one set of plans had been used for every structure with only very slight alterations made for the different requirements of each. Even the base theater, lacking a marquee, had only a row of glass doors across the front to distinguish it from all the other buildings. They were uniformly stucco, painted grayish green, surrounded by neat narrow strips of grass and neat pale squares of concrete sidewalk.

The bus started and stopped, started and stopped. People got on and off, about half in uniform, most of the uniforms the casual workwear of fatigues. Only two officers rode the bus during the time Parker was on it, and both of them seemed to feel out of place.

There was a great deal of coming and going out there, people walking along the sidewalks, going in and out of the buildings, riding by in cars and trucks. Down the cross-streets where the barracks were, lines of cars were angle-parked, other cars moved slowly in the sunlight.

Parker said, "Is there always this much activity?"

"Sure," Devers said. "See, the schools run on three shifts. Six in the morning till noon is A shift. Noon to six, B shift. And six to midnight, C shift. So there's always two-thirds of the students off-duty. And a lot of the permanent party works shifts, too, so some of them are off-duty now."

The finance office was a hell of a distance from the main gate; Parker counted sixteen blocks, with the bus only having made one right and one left turn.

When Devers said, his voice suddenly just a bit more tense, "That's it there," Parker told him:

"We'll wait two blocks, and walk back."

"Good."

They got off the bus two stops later. No one else got off with them, and after the bus pulled away Parker said to Devers, "You better stay here. We don't want your friends inside to look out a window and see you with two guys they don't know."

"I was thinking about that," Devers said. "You're right. So when you go by, the finance offices are on the second floor. The first floor is the Red Cross on the left and the re-enlistment office on the right. Major Creighton's office is way to the left upstairs, that's where the safe is."

"All right. We'll be back in a few minutes."

It was a bright day but cool. It was like walking along the sidewalk in some clean little town, except for the uniforms on so many of the passersby. About a quarter of them were women, some in WAF uniform and some in civilian clothing.

The finance office was in a building like all the rest; two-storey, stucco, rectangular, A-roof, gray-green, casement windows, off-white woodwork. Signs were in the windows flanking the main entrance, which was in the middle of one of the long walls. The signs on the left were dominated by red crosses, those on the right by the word *bonus*. The last two second-storey windows on the left were covered by wire mesh and vertical bars.

Parker and Fusco turned the corner, walked around the building, and saw nothing more except that the second-storey windows all across the left side were also screened with mesh and bars. They walked back to Devers, and Parker said, "Does the finance office work on shifts?"

"Hell, no. Eight to five. Eight to noon on Saturday."

"What about the offices downstairs? The Red Cross open all the time?"

Devers grinned and shook his head. "The Red Cross is shut more than it's open. There's only two people in there, an old guy and a nice-looking chick, and half the time they're down to the snack bar having coffee."

"What about the re-enlistment office?"

"Same hours as us."

Parker nodded, stood looking around. This part of the base was laid out in a grid of streets, every block an absolute square, with two long buildings on each side. Parker said, "Is the whole base set up like this? These streets like this?"

"Mostly. Except around the flight line."

"Can we walk to this other gate?"

"Sure. It's down that way, to the right."

The South Gate turned out to be three blocks from the finance office; one over and two down. It was a smaller gate, less pretentious, with no billboard outside. They stood half a block away and watched a few trucks and cars go in and out. There was no pedestrian traffic at all.

Parker said, "Where's that gate lead to?"

Devers said, "Something called Hilker Road. Down that way it meets up with the road we took out here on the bus. The other way it goes off into the woods someplace. Comes out around Cooks Corners, I think."

"There's no bars out there, no diners, nothing like that?"

"Nothing but woods."

"What about a bus stop?"

"You mean outside? A civilian bus?" Devers shook his head. "The only bus away from here is that one we took out from town, stops at the main gate."

"So there's no reason for anybody to walk off the base in that direction."

Devers looked towards the gate. "I guess not," he said. "I never thought about it, but you're right. You'd only go out that way if you were in a car and this was closer than the main gate."

"What about these trucks coming in?"

"I guess they're headed for places nearer here than the main gate. Maybe there's some kind of shortcut in from the highway, I don't know."

"We'll want to know," Parker said. "We'll want to know what trucks come in, where they go, which ones are regular arrivers, what times of day they come in. We'll want to know what route they take to get here."

Devers said, "That just means sitting and watching for a few days, and then following a couple of trucks away when they leave."

"That's what we'll do, then," Parker said. He looked around. "Is there any building overlooking this that we could get into without any static?"

Devers considered, and then pointed to a building off to the left, the second rank in from the fence. "There's some kind of technical library in there," he said. "You could hang around in there without anybody paying any attention, as long as you kept a book in your hand."

"Good. All right, let's go back." They started walking, and Parker said, "Does that number one bus make a belt? If we get on it, can we go completely around and come back where we started?"

"Sure," said Devers. "They're all belts."

"I want to look at the base," Parker said.

They walked back to the bus stop where they'd gotten off, and when the next bus came along in the same direction they boarded it and sat as before. Devers kept up a low-voiced running description as they went, with Parker asking an occasional question.

It took twenty minutes to get back to the main gate. They got off the bus there and Devers said, "Anything else you want to see?"

"Not today. Let's go back and talk."

"Fine."

They went through the gate without trouble, and there was a civilian bus waiting out by the road. They climbed aboard and a few minutes later the bus started for town.

8

ELLEN FUSCO met them at the door, furious and showing it. "You know my session's at one o'clock," she told Devers.

"I forgot," he said. "Sorry, sweetheart, I was thinking about other things. Here's the keys."

She took them without comment. "Pam's in the yard," she said, and went out to the car.

The three men went into the house and Devers shut the door, saying to Fusco, "If that ex-wife of yours doesn't come off it pretty soon, I'll be trading places with you."

"Ellen wouldn't take me back," Fusco said. "Even if I wanted," he added, and headed for the kitchen. "I need something to eat. Parker?"

"Coffee."

"There should be hamburger," Devers said. "Why don't you make us all some?"

"Coming up," Fusco said, and went on out to the kitchen. A minute later he was moving around out there with an apron on.

Devers said to Parker, "You've got more questions."

"A few now. I'll have more later, when I've thought about it a little more."

"Naturally."

"Sit down," Parker said, and himself went to the chair he'd been sitting in the last time. When Devers was settled on the sofa, Parker said, "The building next door to the finance office, facing the barred windows on the side. What's in there?"

"Legal department," Devers said. "They've got the entire

building and they work eight to five."

"Can you get me a map of the base?"

"Sure. There's one they give the new boys when they arrive, it's only got a few things listed on it, like the Post Office and Supply Building, but we can fill in whatever else we need."

"Good. Do you have a Polaroid?"

"A camera?"

"A Polaroid," Parker insisted. "We don't want any drugstore developing our prints."

"I don't have one myself," Devers said, "but I know a couple guys on base who do. I can borrow one for a day or two."

"Good. I'll want pictures of the finance building, every side. And the offices inside, if you can manage it."

"That could be tricky," Devers said.

"Don't do it if it'll blow things."

"I'll see what I can work out. Anything else?"

"Probably. I'll let you know."

Fusco came walking in with three cups of coffee on a tray, distributed them, said to Devers, "If I was you, I'd quit paying for that analyst of hers. All she does is make you babysit while she's at the sessions."

Devers shrugged, saying, "What the hell. She's nervous about this, that's all. She was married to you when you got yourself caught. She doesn't want to see the same thing happen to me."

"Maybe you ought to be her analyst," Fusco said. "I'll bring the burgers in in a minute."

"Take a look at the kid, will you?" Devers asked him.

"I already did. She's fine."

Fusco went back into the kitchen, and Devers said to Parker, "Is this weird? I'm shacked up with a broad, she's got a kid, her ex-husband is around the place as much as I am, I'm in on a goddam robbery with him, I'm paying for the broad's analysis, I swear to God I never thought I'd get involved in anything this complicated in my life."

"The robbery part is simple," Parker told him. "We look

it over, we see if it can be done, we work out the method, we do it, we split. We don't let other things come in and make complications."

"I follow you," Devers said. "Don't worry, Mis — sorry. Don't worry, anyway. There won't be any complications."

Fusco came back in with the hamburgers, "I been listening," he said. "You think it can be done, Parker?"

"Maybe."

"But it looks good?" Fusco said.

"So far," said Parker.

Part Two

1

"THEY'RE GOING to do it," Ellen said. "I know they're going to do it now." Shivering, she hugged herself and shook her head. "I thought it was just a dream for a long while, just a game they were playing. I thought my husband had learned his lesson, I thought he was too scared to try anything like that again. But it's real, it's going to happen, and this time he's going to take Stan with him."

Dr Godden said, "What makes you so sure?"

"The man who came today," Ellen said. "The man my husband brought back with him from Puerto Rico."

It was easy to talk to Dr Godden. She could fold her arms around herself an look at the intricate patterns in the Persian rug and tell him everything, everything that troubled her. She'd never been able to talk to anybody else like this, never in her life. Certainly not her parents, who listened only to judge, who were never anything in her life but judges, critical judges, prejudiced judges, hanging judges. And certainly not Marty Fusco, whom she now understood she'd married simply as an act of revolt against her parents and who had been no one to understand and help a person like her at all. There was no one, that was the bare fact of it, no one on earth to talk to, no one who would pay attention and try to see and understand and help. Until Dr Fred Godden.

It was the boy before Stan who'd first talked to her about going into analysis, and of course then she'd laughed at the idea, she'd thought analysis was for complicated neurotic people, movie stars and famous writers and society people and like that. Ordinary people like her didn't go to psychoanalysts. But Bert — that was his name — did go to an analyst, because of deep-seated hidden fears that he was homosexual, and eventually he talked Ellen into going to Dr Godden, too. Not long after that, Bert moved to New York City, to Greenwich Village, to try to work out his problem down there, but by then Ellen had learned just how good analysis could be, and she'd kept on with it ever since.

It was Dr Godden who'd helped her get rid of all that leftover guilt she'd been carrying around, not even knowing it was there, weighing her down, making her do things that afterward she knew didn't make any sense, things that only could wind up with her getting hurt again.

Because she'd wanted to get hurt, it was as simple as that. All the guilt her parents had saddled on to her, and then the guilt of feeling that she'd let Marty Fusco down, betrayed him, when she'd divorced him after he was sent away to prison.

But it had been the right thing to do. Because he *hadn't* been the right man for her, he was only a symbol of a revolt that was now complete. She didn't have to do symbolic things against her parents anymore, she was free of them now. So it was right to have divorced Marty, and that was the reason it was right and the real reason she'd done it, though at the time she'd told herself it was because of Pamela.

There was guilt there, too, guilt toward Pamela, feelings of inadequacy and fraudulence. It was all very confused still, very muddled and unclear, but they'd been working on it, hour by hour, three hour-long sessions a week, Monday and Wednesday and Friday, and they'd been getting closer and closer to the root of it all, and then this robbery business had come along, throwing everything out of kilter, and since then it seemed that was all she could ever talk about with Dr Godden.

Particularly in the last week, since Marty had found out where his so-called "organizer" was, at his ease between robberies down there in Puerto Rico, and Stan had offered to pay Marty's plane fare down to talk to this man, this Parker, and bring him back.

And now he was here, and it was real, and it was actually going to happen, and Ellen sat in Dr Godden's office, hugging herself, staring at the complex patterns in the carpet, and felt the heaviness of inevitable disaster weighing down on her like a black raincloud. Because the man had come from Puerto Rico, and it was going to be done.

"Tell me about this man," said Dr Godden. His voice, as always, was soft and gentle, but not at all dramatic like a hypnotist's voice in the movies, the way she'd thought psychoanalysts' voices sounded. And he didn't have a beard, or an accent, or anything like that. He was just an ordinary man, perhaps forty-five , very well-dressed, balding, with a fringe of black hair over his ears and on the back of his head. He wore glasses with pale plastic rims, and he never took notes, and his eyes were unfailingly sympathetic behind his glasses, and if sometimes the hour went over a little he never rushed her, never complained, never cut her off.

She said in answer to his question, "His name is Parker. I don't know what his first name, is, nobody said. I don't like him."

"Why not?"

"He's — I don't know, I look at him and I think *he's evil*. But that isn't right, exactly, I don't think he's evil. I mean, I don't think he'd ever be cruel or anything like that, for the fun of it. I wouldn't worry about leaving Pam around him, for instance. But — I know."

"Yes?"

"He wouldn't hurt Pam, but he wouldn't care about her either. If something bad happened to her, he wouldn't be pleased by it but he wouldn't try to do anything to help her. Unless he saw some gain for himself in it."

"You mean he seems cold?"

"He doesn't *care*. There's no emotion there."

"Oh, well," Dr Godden said, and even though she wasn't looking at him she could hear the gentle smile in his voice, "everyone has emotions. We all have them — you, me, everyone. Even this man Parker. Perhaps he has them bottled up more than most people, that's all."

"That's just the same, then," she said. "If he has them and keeps them inside, it's just the same as not having them at all."

"That's very true. But of course you're seeing this man while he's at work, you might say. Perhaps in Puerto Rico he's a very different kind of man. Perhaps there he relaxes and allows himself to feel his emotions."

She shook her head. "I can't imagine him ever feeling emotions. I can't imagine him crying. Or even laughing."

"Seems to me," Dr Godden said gently, "you've turned this man into some sort of myth figure, something bigger than life."

"I don't know, maybe I have. I suppose I have. Because now it's real, he means it's real, it's going to happen."

"He's the organizer you told me about on Monday."

It always surprised and pleased her when he remembered the things she told him. He had other patients, he was being paid to listen to her, he didn't have to remember, but he did. "Yes, he is," she said. "He came up from Puerto Rico."

"Has he met with Stan?"

"Stan took him out to the base today. That's why I'm late."

"Perhaps this man will decide the job is too difficult. Perhaps he'll tell Stan it can't be done."

She shook her head stubbornly. "They'll do it," she said. "I know they will. I can see it in all their eyes."

"The new man, too?"

"Him especially."

"What do you see in his eyes?"

"I don't know, it's — it's hard to explain. That he's going to do it, that nothing will stop him from doing it."

"Hmmmm. When do they plan it for?"

She shook her head. "I don't know."

"Well, it would be a payday, wouldn't it? Or the day before. When does the Air Force pay again?"

"The fifteenth. Next Tuesday."

"Four days from now," he said. "Can they get ready that quickly?"

"I don't think so," she said. "I remember, with Marty,

it always took a week or two, sometimes more. They don't even have all the men yet. Marty said it would take more than just the three of them."

"So it would probably be the payday after next," Dr Godden said. "The first of October. Let me see, that's a Thursday. Three weeks from yesterday. They probably won't want to stay around this area much longer than that. That is, if you're right and they really intend to do it."

"They'll do it," she said, in the tone of voice she might have used to say, *everybody dies*.

"We have three weeks to find out," Dr Godden said. "But if it's still in such early stages, I don't think you can really be as sure as you are. You know what I think it is?"

"The same old thing," she said, smiling a bit shyly at the pattern in the carpet, knowing what he was going to say.

"You tell me," he said, urging her gently.

"It's the feeling of being undeserving," she said. "The feeling that I don't deserve to have anything good, so I won't get anything good. I'm sure they'll do it because I'm sure they'll get caught and then I won't have Stan. Because I don't deserve Stan." She sneaked a quick look at him, saw his sympathetic face, his balding head gleaming in the light. Looking quickly back at the carpet she said, "I know that's part of it. But that isn't the whole thing. I mean, Marty *did* get caught."

"Once," Dr Godden said. "And how many times did he commit robberies and not get caught?"

"Oh, lots," she said. She was no longer amazed at how easily she could talk with Dr Godden about robberies and criminals. It was almost as though he were a priest; different, but sympathetic, never judging, never condemning, never trying to force her to conform to what society might want. How many people could she talk to about Marty, be truthful, tell them her ex-husband was a robber, it was his profession? Most people would be shocked, they'd want to call the police or at least to stop having anything to do with her. But Dr Godden took everything just the same; calm and understanding, and without judging. She could talk to him about anything, about sex or Marty or her parents or anything at all, and it was never a problem.

Now, calm as ever, Dr Godden was saying, "Then there's no reason to believe they'll be caught this time. After all, Stan is the only one among them who isn't a professional at this sort of thing."

"But even if they don't get caught this time," she said, exploring her fear further now, "it won't be any good. Stan will want to do it again, he'll want to become like Marty. Or like the other man, Parker."

"I see," Dr Godden said. "You're afraid Stan will turn out to be your first husband again."

She nodded rapidly, frowning at the rug.

"That's a not unusual fear among girls in your situation," Dr Godden said. "But frankly, from what you've told me of Stan I think it more likely one taste of that sort of life will be more than enough for him. Who knows, the experience might be good for him, he might come out of it much more likely husband material than he went in."

It was wonderful how Dr Godden always found a calmer way to look at things, a more pleasant way. And a lot of the time his way turned out to be right, and all her fears and doubts and premonitions turned out to be nothing but the old insecurity again, the old inadequacy and unworthiness.

"I guess," she said hesitantly, "I guess the only thing we can do now is wait."

"That's all," agreed Dr Godden.

2

STAN TOOK a shot of the vault, peeled the print out of the back of the camera, saw it had come out as well as the rest, and strolled on back to his desk. He tucked the photo into the envelope in his center drawer with the rest, put the camera back in the side drawer, and was typing away like sixty when Lieutenant Wormley came back in from the head.

"Don't work so hard," Wormley said on his way by. "It's only Saturday."

"Yes, sir," said Stan. Wormley was a fuzzy-faced chinless wonder, an ROTC second lieutenant two years younger than Stan. He continued on down the rows of desks now, went into his own glass-enclosed cubicle next to Major Creighton's office, and buried his face again in *Scientific American*. Stan had taken all his pictures except the vault shot while Wormley was lost strayed or stolen inside that magazine.

Sergeant Novato had been tougher to work around. A tough, compact little man who'd never expected assignment anywhere that required brainwork, he took the tasks of this office a hell of a lot more seriously than anybody else, and on the Saturdays when he was on duty he got more accomplished than most people did in a full eight-hour weekday. But it was his very busyness that had helped Stan to shoot around him. When Novato was bouncing around the files, in and out of one drawer after another, pulling this file, putting that file back, Stan got his pictures of the other end of the office. And when Novato was down there, absorbed in arithmetic at his desk, Stan took his pictures in the other direction.

He'd already taken care of the exterior shots and the staircase on the way in, and the shot of the vault through the window of Major Creighton's office finished the pictures he wanted from here. So now all he had to do was wait for twelve o'clock — another interminable forty-five minutes away — and then drive around the base a little to get the rest of the pictures Parker wanted. He'd be home by one-thirty at the latest.

It was a good thing Lanz had gone along with the switch. Otherwise it would have been tough to get these pictures for Parker. But Lanz had been happy to switch Saturdays with Stan — just to put off his own duty day — so here he was, and the pictures were done.

Nobody seeemed to know why the Saturday morning skeleton staff was required, but then nobody seemed to know why the Air Force wanted almost anything done the way they did. It was just a fact of life, that's all; on Saturday mornings one officer, one non-com and one airman had to be on duty from eight till noon. It was less trouble on the lower ranks than on the officers and non-coms, since there were more airmen to divvy up the duty among themselves, but it was still an occasional pain in the ass.

Stan's next duty wasn't scheduled for another five weeks, but Jerry Lanz had agreed to switch with him, and the two other people on duty this morning had turned out, in their separate ways, to be perfect for what Stan had in mind. He'd done a small amount of typing, a large amount of picture-taking, and all in all he considered the morning, unlike most of these stinking Saturdays, well spent.

Stan was enjoying all of this, the preparation, the talk, the gathering of professionals, the gearing up methodically and matter-of-factly for the one grand profitable moment of high drama. He had felt an affinity with Marty Fusco from the first, despite the difference in their ages, and that feeling was even stronger now with Parker. Parker was a man he would follow. He had seen and understood Parker's mistrust of him when they'd first met, and had been delighted at the gradual shift in Parker's attitude, until now he was sure

Parker's acceptance of him was almost complete.

That he should find his place at last at the side of a man like Parker didn't surprise Stan Devers at all. For as long as he could remember he'd been a swimmer upstream, a rebel for the sake of rebellion, anti rules and anti dullness and anti everything that plain stolid ordinary society was for. He'd been thrown out of two high schools and one college — having already, in college, been thrown out of ROTC — he'd been fired from most of the jobs he'd ever held, and that he was surviving four years of Air Force regimentation without earning himself either a Bad Conduct or Undesirable Discharge sometimes amazed him. His troubles in the past had ranged from insubordination through constant absences to the theft of one high school teacher's car — for a joyride only — and that he had held his natural tendencies in check for three and a half military years now meant not that he'd reformed but that he'd understood at once that the Air Force was a tougher proposition than any school. Hit a teacher and the worst you could get was thrown out. Hit an officer and they'd put you in *jail* for five years.

His mother had started prophesying jail for him years ago, when he was still in high school. Everything Stan had told Parker about his mother was true; they'd never gotten along and never would. She was now either on her fourth husband or looking for her fifth, he didn't know or care which. Although he hadn't really ever given his grandmother — or anybody else — any money, she had truly been the only relative he'd ever had any kind of friendly relationship with, and her death last year had hit him harder than he'd thought anything like that could do. He was now a loner partly by choice and partly by chance, and his being shacked up with Ellen Fusco didn't to his way of thinking change his loner status a bit. If Ellen thought marriage was somewhere in their future, it wasn't because he'd ever encouraged the notion. Nor had he contradicted it; it kept her generally tractable.

Until recently, that is. Until this robbery business had come up. Ever since then she'd been a truculent bitch, grousing around like some soap-opera Cassandra, snapping his head off at the slightest pretext. If he'd ever had any idea of taking her with him when he got out of the service, the last couple of weeks had put the kibosh on that. You'd think psychoanalysis would have made her more sensible.

Stan was brooding about this so much he forgot to look at the clock, and the next thing he knew Lieutenant Wormley was coming by his desk, rolled-up magazine in his hand, grinning and saying, "Stan, you're becoming a positive company man. If the Major could only see you now."

"Yes, sir," Stan said. "I'm bucking for civilian." There was a time when it would have grated on him to call a little punk like Wormley "sir", but by now the word was automatic. It was one of the painless little things you did to get by, you called the Wormley's "sir". And if "sir" had one definition for the Wormleys and another definition for Stan, a private definition all his own, that was Stan's business.

Wormley had to lock up. He stood waiting at the door while Stan and Sergeant Novato got ready. Stan put the camera and the envelope full of photos into a brown paper bag and headed for the door.

Wormley nodded at the bag. "Taking home samples, Stan?"

"You bet, sir." You bet, you simple son of a bitch.

3

STAN TOOK pictures of the office," Ellen said.

"Oh?" Dr Godden's voice expressed polite interest. "Why did he do that?"

"I don't know. That man Parker wanted him to. All kinds of pictures, not just of the office."

"What else?"

"Oh, the gate, and the outside of the building where he works, and some trucks and buses and things."

"Well, well" said Dr Godden. "It does sound as though they're serious, doesn't it?"

"I knew they were."

"It seems you were right," said Dr Godden. "Are they hiding their plans from you?"

"No, How could they, they're using my house! As though I *wanted* to know what they were doing."

"Don't you?"

"I do not," she told the carpet. "When they start talking, I leave the room right away."

"Why is that?"

"I hate it!" she burst out, glaring at the patterns in the carpet. "I hate the thought of it, I hate everything they're doing."

"Is it only because you're afraid they'll be caught, or that Stan will want to keep doing it until he does get caught?"

"I don't know. How do I know?" She knew she was getting agitated, but she couldn't help it. "I just hate them being there, doing all that – all that."

"Well, let's think about it," he said. "You say you hate

them being there, making their preparations in your house. Is that the point? That it's your house?"

"I don't know. I suppose it could be."

"Do you feel they are violating your hospitality? Or that Stan is betraying you somehow, entering into a plan with your ex-husband?"

"I don't think so," she said, frowning at the carpet, trying to think, trying to see if anything Dr Godden was saying found a response inside her. He did that sometimes, offered one reason for a thing after another until they found the one she responded to, and that was usually it. Even if the response was strongly negative. In fact, if she were to say *definitely no* to something, nine times out of ten that would turn out to be what the reason was after all.

"Do you object," he asked her now, "to your husband using your home? Or is this planning just reminiscent of the times when you were married to him, particularly the time when he did get caught?"

"Yes," she said. She looked briefly directly at him, at those intelligent sympathetic eyes, and then away again.

"That's it," she said, knowing it was. "It makes me nervous, them all in the living-room, just the way it used to be. I feel, I feel trapped, as though nothing was changed, I'm not really free of Marty after all."

"Of course," he agreed. "The reminiscence is there, the similarity with the past. But there are differences, you know."

"Yes, I know."

"You are free of your ex-husband. He is there only on your sufferance. That's a big difference, isn't it?"

"Sometimes I think I ought to tell them to go someplace else."

"No!"

He said it so forcefully she was surprised into looking at him again. For just a second his expression seemed to be startled, but then it smoothed again and he said, "Ellen, you can't run away from things. We've talked about that before."

"Yes," she said, and faced front again. "I know. You're

right."

"You should let them stay," he said. "You should face the problem squarely, understand it, conquer it."

"I know."

"In fact," he said, "you shouldn't run away from their meetings. You should be present as much as they permit. You should listen to everything they say, you should know just as much of their plans as they do." He paused, and said, "Do you know why?"

"To help me understand why I'm afraid?"

"That too, of course. But even more than that, you should know precisely what they plan to do, because if the plan *is* a good one you'll be spared a great deal of unnecessary worry. Who knows, if you listened to what they have in mind you might find out it's really a very good and safe plan, and then you'd have one less problem to worry about. Wouldn't you?"

She smiled at the carpet. "I guess I would."

"You can talk their plans over with me," he told her. "Together we'll try and decide if they can get away with what they intend to do."

"What if we don't think they can?" she asked.

"Then we'll decide why," he said. "We'll discuss their ideas, and if we see things that look like flaws you can show them to Stan, either so they'll make their plan better or so he'll decide not to go ahead with it."

"I don't dare tell Stan," she said, "that I've been talking about all this with you."

"That's understandable."

"He wouldn't believe I'm perfectly safe telling you anything," she said. She looked at him, actually held his eyes this time. "Anything at all," she said.

His smile was gentle, sympathetic. "I'm pleased you have confidence in me," he said.

4

FUSCO PULLED the Pontiac into the cinder driveway beside the house. There was no garage, only the driveway, ending at a metal fence. The fence completely enclosed the back yard, which was perfect for Pam. The kid was out there every warm and rainless day, with the whole yard to roam in. A hell of a lot more than the chunk of Canarsie pavement Fusco had had when he was a kid.

Fusco shut the Pontiac door and walked over to the fence. There was Pam, all the way at the other end of the yard, squatting the way little kids do, digging in the dirt back there with a tablespoon Ellen had given her.

Ellen was a good mother, there was no denying it. Yeah, and she'd been a good wife, too. It was him that was off. As a husband he'd been punk, and as a father he was the kind of guy who could show up once a year with a balloon and a box of Cracker Jack and other than that have no idea what the hell he was supposed to do. It was a good thing Pam had a mother like Ellen.

The one thing Fusco couldn't work out entirely was his feeling about Stan. It seemed to him he ought to be bugged by it one way or another. Stan shacked up with Ellen, but when he thought about it he didn't feel bugged at all. What the hell, they weren't married any more. And after three years in the pen, completely separated from her, he had practically no emotional involvement left for Ellen at all any more. Oh, a little, but he thought that was mostly because of the kid, because she was the one in charge of bringing up his daughter.

He liked to look at Pam. He liked to know she was there. But he shouldn't hang around out here too long now. Without having called to the child or in any way attracted her attention, Fusco moved away from the fence, walked around the Pontiac, and went into the house by the front door.

It was a little after six, and Ellen was in the kitchen making dinner. Parker was sitting on the sofa, looking at Stan's pictures spread out on the coffee table. Stan wasn't around.

Parker looked up. "It work out?"

"Beautiful," Fusco told him. "I sat at a table right next to a window, I could see everything happened at the gate. I had a book open in front of me, my notebook open, it looked like I was copying down stuff I was reading. Nobody paid me any attention at all."

Stan came in from the bedroom then, saying, "Marty, tomorrow I get my car back. I hate that stinking bus."

"I was going to be there longer than you," Fusco reminded him.

"I know, I know." Stan looked at Parker. "You want to go over his stuff now, or after dinner?"

"Whenever Fusco's ready," Parker said.

"Couple minutes," Fusco said. He dropped his notebook on an end table and went into the bathroom to wash up for dinner. He didn't know why, but sitting in that library all day had made him stiff; his back creaked when he bent over the sink to wash his face.

When he came out, Parker and Stan had moved to the kitchen table and Ellen was dishing up supper. Parker and Fusco both were taking most of their meals here, but were sleeping elsewhere, Fusco at the residence hotel over Checkers' Bar & Grill down on Front Street, Parker at the motel in Malone, fifteen miles away. Parker had the Pontiac every night, but always brought it back in the morning in time for Stan to take it to the base. Unless, like this morning, either Parker or Fusco had a use for the car.

Fusco sat down at the table and Ellen put a plate in front of him without a word, meatloaf, green beans, boiled potato. Starving, Fusco dug right in.

When Ellen sat down she said to Fusco, "How was your day?"
"Good," he told her. "No trouble at all."
"That's good," she said. In the last couple of days she'd gotten a lot better, a lot easier to get along with. She'd been all up in the air about this caper for a long time, but now all that seemed changed. Maybe she'd grown resigned to it, or maybe she'd just gotten interested in how the score was shaping up. Ever since Monday she'd been fine, listening to them talking things over, not bitching about anything. Stan had been understandably more relaxed himself as a result.
Fusco liked it when people were relaxed. He hated trouble in the air, interpersonal hang-ups. It was much better now, the four of them sitting around the kitchen table together, Stan telling funny stories about some kid second lieutenant in his office. Fusco had two helpings of everything.
Afterwards, back in the living-room, Fusco reported on his day, giving the names and times of all the commercial vehicles in and out of the South Gate, the quantity of passenger cars at different times of day, what Air Force vehicles used that gate in and out. At the end he said, "There were two trucks went out that gate but didn't come in, at least not while I was there. One was a garbage truck, green, said S & L Sanitation Service on the side, went through at three-twenty. The other was a Pepsi-Cola truck, went through at four thirty-five. I figure they both must of come in the main gate, went through some kind of set route, and then they go out this way."
Parker said, "What kind of check do the commercial trucks get?"
"They must have some kind of pass," Fusco told him. "Every one of them stopped, the driver held something out for the kid on the gate to look at, and then the kid waved him through."
"In and out both?"
"Right."
"Nobody got waved through? Not even people going to be the same every day? The gate guards have to know some

of those drivers."

Fusco shook his head. "Everybody stopped. No exceptions."

Stan told Parker, "There's some chicken outfit goes around trying to crack security on Air Force bases. They hit here three or four months ago, and the story went all over the base. One of their men came in in a Coke company truck, put a red brick with 'bomb' stenciled on it in white in every Coke machine on the base. Then called up the Provost Marshal and told him the whole base had just blown up."

Parker shook his head. "That's beautiful. So now they're bright and alert. Just to make things tougher."

Fusco said. "We wouldn't count on them being slack anyway. It doesn't change anything." He still had a small fear that Parker would suddenly decide the job was no good after all, and up and walk out. Parker was capable of something like that, if he didn't like the set-up.

But it wasn't going to happen now, not over the gate guards. Parker nodded agreeement with what Fusco had said, and turned to Stan, saying, "What time does the payroll get to the base?"

"To the base, or to our office?"

"Both. Base first."

"The plane lands at nine-twenty. The money gets into the finance office no later than quarter to ten."

"When does it start getting split up?"

"Right away. Six guys work on it all day long."

"They work after hours?"

Stan grinned. "No, they get it done by five. I know, I'm one of the six, all we want is to be done and out of there by five o'clock."

"Where's this happen?"

Stan picked up one of the photos on the coffee table and handed it over to Parker. "In the Major's office there. Where the vault is. See those two long tables along the left wall? That's where we sit."

"And the two boxes with the money?"

"In front," Stan said. "Next to the glass wall here."

"Is that glass bulletproof?"

"No, it's just regular plate glass."

"But the windows back here are barred."

Stan shrugged. "That's the way the Air Force does things."

Ellen came quietly in at that point, carrying a cup of coffee for herself, and sat unobtrusively in the chair in the corner.

Parker said, "Besides the six men working on the payroll, who else is upstairs then?"

"Everybody who works up there," Stan said. "About twenty people."

"Anybody else in the room with the money?"

"The Major. And Lieutenant Wormley and Captain Henley. They both check out .45's from Supply in the morning and stand around and play guard."

"Describe them."

"Wormley and Henley?" Stan shrugged. "Wormley's like his name. A little creep, fresh out of ROTC. A nothing."

"What about Henley?"

"He's supposed to be an alcoholic," Stan said. "I don't know. He lives with his family in the dependent housing area, he's got lots of kids, he's in his forties, I hear he was passed over for major once, he likes to reminisce about when he was in Europe in the Second World War."

"Does he know how to use a gun?"

Stan shrugged. "Beats me. All officers are supposed to be checked out on the .45. I figure Wormley just went to the firing range and shut his eyes and plugged away till they told him to stop. Maybe Henley did do some stuff in the Big War, I don't know."

Fusco had been listening, trying to figure out the characters of the men from Stan's descriptions. He was pretty good at that, at working out what kind of a man somebody was and guessing what that kind of man would do in such a situation. Now he said, "That's the one to look out for. Henley."

Stan didn't understand. He looked at Fusco and said, "The war was a long time ago."

"Not for anything he learned in the war," Fusco said. "If he's a passed-over captain, maybe twenty-five years in the service, got a family, drinks too much, maybe he's out to prove himself. Maybe he'd like to be a hero and make major."

Stan squinted, thinking about it. "Henley? You just could be right. He does get belligerent sometimes."

Parker said, "What about the Major? Who's he?"

"Major Creighton," Stan said. "Kind of a nice guy, grandfather type, easygoing, got a little white moustache. The WAFs say he's always trying to cop a feel, but all I know is he sits in his office and looks at everybody working and doesn't seem to give much of a damn."

Parker said, "No other guards?"

"Not during the day. They come on at five o'clock, when we quit. I think they work two shifts, they must change around midnight or something. I'm not sure how that works."

"All right. What time does the money leave the next morning?"

"First thing. About five or ten after eight. It goes down into the armored car and that's the end of it."

"The question is," said Fusco, "do we want to go after it in the daytime the day before, or wait until night?"

"We can't decide that yet," Parker said.

"Yes we can," said Stan. "You'll have to do it in the daytime. You don't dare try to move around that base at night. Besides, in the daytime all the guards are Wormley and Henley. Whatever Henley's like, he's an amateur at being a guard. At night, you've got APs to tackle, inside and out."

"If we do it in the daytime," Parker told him, "and there's static, you'll have to play it like we aren't on your team. And we'll have to play it that way, too."

"You won't have to gun me down," Stan said, grinning.

"I know that. But you want to be there in uniform when we do it, with twenty witnesses around?"

"I'll just stand there with my hands up," Stan said, and stuck his hands into the air.

Fusco said, "Stan's right, the daytime is our only chance.

At least, that's what I think."

Parker seemed to be considering it. He picked up a couple of the photos, looked at them, put them down. "A daylight haul is tougher," he said. "Let's let it ride for a while. We'll figure either way, day or night, we're going to need three more men, including a driver. That's six men, equal shares. You say there's four hundred grand in the kitty?"

Stan said, "About that. A little more, a little less, it changes every payday."

"About sixty-five thousand each," Fusco said.

"We can build up an A string for that," Parker said. He looked at Fusco. "You got any ideas?"

Fusco had. "There was a guy I met on the inside," he said. "He was only in because he was finked on. He'd be out by now. He looked solid and dependable, and he knew a lot of the same guys we do."

"What's his name?"

"Jake Kengle."

Parker shook his head. "I don't know him. You know how to get in touch with him?"

"He gave me an address before I got out."

"Give him a try. You know Philly Webb?"

"Sure," said Fusco. "He drove for me once in Norfolk, he's a good man."

"I'll contact him," Parker said.

Fusco said, "What about that foreign guy? Salsa. He still around?"

"Dead," Parker said, "Couple of years ago."

From her corner, Ellen surprisingly said, "Bill Stockton's always good."

"That's right," Fusco said. To Parker he said, "You remember Stockton, don't you? Tall, skinny as a flagpole, black hair straight up on top of his head. Sharpshooter."

"I remember him," Parker said. "You want to contact him, or should I?"

"I'll do it," Fusco said. "You see about financing."

Stan said, "Financing? What's that?"

Fusco explained to him: "We'll have expenses beforehand.

guns, maybe. A car, other things. We get financing from somebody outside, he gets back double if the caper works."

"Why don't we finance ourselves?"

Parker said, "If the money man is involved it tends to make for trouble. He starts acting like he's got extra votes. It's better to have it done on the outside."

Fusco said, "The reason I thought you ought to handle that, Parker, money men tend to shy away from somebody been on the inside. Superstitious or something."

"I'll take care of it," Parker said. To Stan he said, "How can we mount a night watch on the South Gate, same as what Fusco just did?"

"That's easy," Stan said. "I just sit there in a car. Nobody'll bother about me."

"We'll need it from eleven-thirty tonight till about four tomorrow morning," Parker said.

"Tonight?" Stan's grin turned pained. "I forgot," he said, "about never volunteering."

Fusco said, "I'll come long if you want, Stan, help keep you company."

Stan pointed a finger at him. "You just volunteered, pal," he said.

Parker said, "One of you can drive me back to the motel first, and come pick me up in the morning."

Ellen said, "You could stay here tonight." There was nothing suggestive in her voice, or in her face when Fusco looked at her, nothing but a flat statement and an expressionless face, but Fusco felt the shock go through the room, felt Stan tensing, felt himself going taut, and he was amazed at how relieved he was when Parker answered, just as flatly, "I'd rather stick to the routine."

Fusco got to his feet, suddenly in a hurry to break up this meeting. "I'll take you, Parker," he said.

"Good," Parker said, "See you in the morning, Stan."

"See you," said Stan. The moment was over.

5

"Do you know what strikes me as significant?" Dr Godden said.

Ellen had been silent the last three or four minutes, just sitting there with her arms around herself, her eyes fixed on the patterns in the carpet, her mind churning as she tried to find something to talk about and there continued to be nothing, nothing at all. Dr Godden always told her not to worry about the silences, to be silent when she felt like being silent and talk only when she felt like talking, but she hated to have the time go by and her not saying anything to him, not accomplishing anything with him. They'd done so much good together already she was impatient to get on with the job, to accomplish everything, to make everything as good as it could possibly be.

This was one of the few times he'd ever broken into one of her silences, and it surprised her almost enough to make her look at him. She checked the head movement in time, turned it into a negative shake, and said, "No, I don't."

"You can't think of anything to talk about," he said. "And I would guess that's because you're trying very hard *not* to think about a particular subject. Do you think that's possible?"

"I don't know," she said, though the suggestion did make her tense. "I can't think of any subject."

"You can't? Well, here it is Monday the twenty-first, and do you know the last time you mentioned the robbery to me? Exactly one week ago. Last Monday. Not a word since then. Wednesday you talked about your mother, Friday you talked about your baby, and today you haven't been able to talk about anything. But the robbery is a scant ten days away, and up until last Monday it was a very strong and important subject to you."

He stopped talking and that meant she had to say something, had to respond in some way. She searched frantically for words, finally muttered, "I don't know, I guess I just don't have anything to say about it any more."

"Have you been attending their meetings, as I suggested?"

"Yes."

"Listening to their plans?"

"Yes."

"Isn't that something to talk about? Their plans?"

"I guess so." She shrugged awkwardly, her face twisted by concentration. "I guess I just don't want to think about it anymore," she said.

"You mean you *don't* listen to their plans?"

"Yes, I do."

"Then you still are interested, you do still think about it. But you don't want to talk about it. Why do you suppose that is?"

"I don't know," she said.

He began to throw out hypotheses, the way he always did. "Could it be because you don't trust me? Or because you now think the plan will work and you were foolish to have worried so much? Or because you now feel attraction again for your husband? Or perhaps for the other man, Parker?"

"No!" she said, so loudly and abruptly she surprised herself. Then she sat there and listened to the word, echoing and reverberating and revealing her to herself, and she saw that she had been staring at one corner of carpet because a line there, a series of lines there, reminded her vaguely of Parker's face in profile, cold and hard and aloof.

"What is Parker to you?" Dr Godden said, "Is he the parent, the stern parent? Is he the father?"

"Cold," she said, not entirely sure if she meant Parker or herself or both, or even how many different ways she might mean it about either of them.

"The one you don't deserve?"

"Wednesday," she said, talking in a monotone, almost a whisper, "Stan was going to be out all night. I asked Parker to stay overnight. I didn't make it sexy, I just asked him. I didn't know that's what I meant, but it was. I'm not sure if he knew."

"Did he stay?"

"No. He left, and I felt relieved. I was glad he hadn't stayed, but I'd had to ask him."

"You were relieved to discover you were still unworthy?"

"I suppose so, I'm not sure."

"What do you feel about this man Parker now?"

"I think I hate him," she said. "I'm afraid of him."

"Because he would be justified in punishing you for your hatred," he suggested. "Because he has done nothing to you directly to justify your hating him. That's why you're afraid, the fear is a way of feeling guilt."

Sometimes the answers were too complicated for her. All she could do now was shake her head.

"Perhaps on Wednesday," he said, "you'll feel like talking about the robbery again. Perhaps you'll understand your feelings better then."

"I'll talk about it now," she said. "Now that I understand this, I want to talk about it, honestly."

"There's no time now," he said, and his voice didn't sound quite as sympathetic as usual. "We'll see what happens on Wednesday."

Now she did feel guilty. She'd been keeping the plans from Dr Godden for no reason, making him feel she didn't trust him, causing a rift between them just when she needed him the most. "I'll tell you the whole thing on Wednesday," she promised.

"If you feel like it," he said.

6

NORMAN BERRIDGE surveyed the body and found it good. The rouge on the cheeks was perhaps a trifle too noticeable, particularly for a sixty-three-year-old man, but relatives tended not to be overly particular about things like that. Just so none of the lip stitching showed or anything actually disastrous along that line, almost any kind of slapdash cosmetology was acceptable. And with the kind of assistant one had to rely on these days, that was just as well.

Ah, well, no need to raise a fuss. It *was* acceptable. Good, in fact. He said so to the assistant standing proudly beside the body, a young Puerto Rican apprentice — Puerto Ricans were about the only ones who would accept proper apprentice wages any more, in this mollycoddled twentieth-century USA — who accepted the compliment with a good deal of pleased hand-fluttering and head-bowing, while his own cheeks got as red as the corpse's.

The wall phone in the corner buzzed. Norman Berridge walked around remains and assistant, picked up the phone, and his secretary said, "There's a man here to see you, Mr Berridge. He says his name is Lynch, he says it's about the annuities."

Berridge pursed his lips. He recognized the name, and the use of the word "annuities". Lynch was one of the men who came to him from time to time for financing of their activities. It was pleasant to have an area of investment offering — at some financial risk, of course — one hundred per cent profit and no involvement other than the initial outlay, but the men with whom he dealt in these matters never failed to unnerve him, and Lynch was possibly the most unnerving of them all. A cold man, as self-contained and silent as a panther, he seemed to Berridge always to be looking on him with contempt for his flabby body and bad nerves and jumbled mind. Lynch himself was as clean and cold and empty as the interior of a new coffin.

Lynch was not of course the man's real name. One time when he had come with another man, the other had called him by a different name, which Berridge could no longer be sure he remembered. Porter, Walker, Archer. . . something like that.

No matter. It wasn't the man's name that counted, it was the opportunity he presented for investment. "I'll be right up," Berridge said into the phone, hung it up, and turned back to see the assistant dabbing at his body's cheek, apparently having himself noticed it was a bit too red for someone not a habitué of Moulin Rouge. "Very good," Berridge said. "Very good."

He turned away from the assistant's redoubled smile of pleasure and went over to the elevator, a small cage barely large enough for two. Shutting the gate, riding up to the main floor, Berridge reminded himself of his frequent vow to start using the stairs. Exercise was all he needed, and soon he'd have back the body of his twenties. Exercise, and some small restraint in diet. Nothing to it.

But he didn't want to be panting when he walked into the room containing Lynch. Next time he was in the basement would be soon enough to start the new regimen. For now, his self-possession in Lynch's presence would be greatly improved if his breathing were normal. Thus, the elevator.

Lynch was standing by the window when Berridge entered his office, gazing without expression at the formal garden Mrs Berridge maintained behind the house. It seemed to Berridge that Lynch never sat down, that their infrequent meetings in this office were always held with Lynch on his feet, as hard as a post.

This time, Berridge decided, he would also remain standing. It would make up a bit for the elevator.

"Lynch," he said, as though pleased to see the man. "It's been quite some time." The false amiability and unction he had learned in dealing with bereaved relatives stood him well in other situations as well, most particularly this one. None of his true ambivalence about Lynch — money versus discomfort — showed in his voice or face.

Lynch turned away from the window, nodded briefly, and said, "I need three thousand."

There was no small talk in Lynch, no social nicety. The man was as stripped and purposeful as a racing car or a fighter plane.

Which was just as well, actually. The last thing Berridge wanted was to know the specifics of the usage to which his money was to be put, and the next to the last thing was idle conversation with this man over some standard subject like the weather.

So Berridge, ordinarily an expansive and loquacious man, matched Lynch's brevity with his own, saying, "No problem at all. The usual terms, I suppose?"

"Right. If it comes off, you'll hear in about ten days."

"About the first of the month?"

"Just after. Second or third, something like that."

"Excellent. You want it now, I suppose."

"Yes."

"Care to come with me to the bank?"

Lynch nodded, and moved away from the window. Berridge, pleased with himself for not having seated himself behind his mahogany desk, led the way out of the office and down the rear hall to the garage, where he pushed the button that opened the third door along, the one for the Toronado. Past that was his daughter's Mustang, while on this side were the Cadillac and his wife's Volkswagen. The hearse and flower car were kept in another garage, beside the house.

Berridge felt good behind the wheel of his Toronado, young and vital. He had noticed that just about every other Toronado driver he had ever seen was, like himself, middle-aged and portly, but this didn't interfere with the illusion of youth the car gave him. He was as capable of doublethink as anyone.

His money, for instance. He considered himself an honest and upright and patriotic man, he detested beatniks and peaceniks and other antisocial freaks as much as anyone, and if his income-tax statements were annual pieces of remarkably baroque fiction that was no contradiction at all, but merely another facet of his character, the hardheaded businessman facet. Poorer families tended to pay morticians in cash; cash was untraceable; untraceable income would only be reported by fools; Norman Berridge was nobody's fool. If in a safety-deposit box in a bank downtown there were wads of wrinkled bills, just as they had come to him from the hands of his clientele, that was simply one way of an ordinary person's defending himself from the encroachments of Big Government.

And if that money was occasionally doubled — and occasionally lost, too — by investment in the unspecified activities of men like Lynch, so what? Since when was investment a crime?

There was no conversation on the ride downtown. Berridge was painfully conscious of Lynch on the seat beside him, but he knew none of the awareness or discomfort showed. He drove, a little too slowly and too cautiously, through the slight mid-morning traffic, angle-parked the car at a parking meter just down the block from the bank, and said, "I'll be right back."

Lynch said nothing to that, which was typical of the man.

Berridge agonized over whether or not to put a dime in the meter. Would Lynch consider him effete if he did, or slovenly if he didn't? Contempt seemed possible in either case.

The problem was solved for him when he put his hand in his change pocket; he had no dimes. He walked on by the meter and down to the bank.

He enjoyed the complexity involved in reaching his box, the gates to be gone through, the form to sign, the dignified obsequiousness of the guard, the necessity of both the guard's key and his own being inserted in the box at the same time.

It all gave him a feeling of importance, and of safety. And the value so obviously conferred on his safety deposit box seemed to rub off on him as well, giving him a feeling that he himself was considered valuable. All in all, a satisfying experience and a welcome antidote to ten minutes in the silent company of Lynch.

Berridge requested and got a large manila envelope. Carrying this and his box, he entered one of the private chambers, sat at the table there, and counted out fifties and twenties and an occasional ten until he had reached three thousand. The bills stuffed the manila envelope, which he could barely seal shut. Then there was the reverse procedure to go through, returning the box to its place and himself to the outside air.

When he returned to the car, Lynch was smoking, the air inside the car acrid with the smell of smoke. Unobstrusively Berridge turned on the air conditioner when he started the engine. Meantime Lynch ripped open the envelope and began to count the bills. He counted as Berridge drove homeward again, his absorption undisturbed by Berridge's progress through the streets. Each little handful, when counted, went into another of Lynch's pockets until when he was done, the envelope was empty, the money was out of sight, and Lynch looked exactly the same as before.

When Berridge was stopped by a red light, Lynch extended a crumpled twenty towards him, saying, "You counted wrong."

"I did?" Surprised, Berridge took the bill, and didn't notice the light had turned green until the car behind him sounded its horn. Then he drove the rest of the way with the bill clutched in his right hand.

When they reached the house — large, white stucco, with well-tended plantings all around and a discreet black-with-gray-letters sign on the lawn — Lynch said, "Let me off in front."

"Certainly."

Lynch didn't say goodbye. Berridge watched him cross the street and get into a Pontiac with a New York State plate.

Stolen? He had no idea.

After Lynch drove away, Berridge drove the Toronado back into the garage, the door opening for him at his approach. Once inside, seeing the manila envelope crumpled on the seat beside him, he permitted himself to become annoyed at Lynch, at his silence, his cold arrogance, his sloppiness in leaving that envelope there.

Berridge looked at the twenty-dollar bill still in his hand. Lynch had only counted the money once. Why had he been so sure it was Berridge who had made the error?

Berridge's stomach felt bad.

7

"I'M NOT upset about Parker any more," Ellen said.

"Oh? Very good."

"All I feel for him now is dislike," she said, and she knew her voice was calm with her certainty.

"I'm glad things are simpler now," Dr Godden said. "What made the change?"

"Different things," she said. "I know that. There was a time when I would have known only one of them, but now I know there's others."

"What's the one you would have known?"

"What he did with the guns," she said. Then, realizing she'd started somewhere in the middle and he couldn't possibly know what she was talking about, she hurried on, "You remember Wednesday I told you he'd gone somewhere and gotten a lot of money. The money to finance things."

"Yes. I found that very interesting. The reasons for getting the financing on the outside and so on."

"Well, yesterday," she said, "he got the guns. They're in toy boxes, model auto racing sets and like that."

"How many guns?"

"Two machine guns and four pistols. All so innocent, packed up in toy boxes. Stan said he got them from a man who runs a hobby shop as a cover for selling illegal guns."

"And the guns bothered you?"

"Not the guns," she said. "What he did with them."

"What did he do with them?"

"He put them on the shelf in Pam's closet." Ellen closed her eyes, hugged herself closer. She could see them sitting there, on the shelf in her baby's room, surrounded by truly innocent toys, all that lethal metal hidden away inside cardboard boxes covered with bright colors and gay lettering and pictures of happy things.

"Don't you see?" she said, but she kept her own eyes closed. "He's using *Pam*. Not just me, not just my house or Stan or even Marty. He's using *Pam,* making her innocence hide his — *filth*."

"You feel violated," Dr Godden suggested.

She opened her eyes, studied the patterned carpet as though the twisting lines would only form letters and words and sentences if she could but look at them right, as though the carpet could tell her something of great importance that would make everything clear and easy and possible. But the pattern remained only twisting lines.

"Not violated," she said, "not exactly violated. It's as though I didn't matter, as though whether I was even alive or not had no meaning at all. He doesn't *care*. I'm a worm to him, less than a worm. Nothing to him. Not even worth feeling contempt toward."

"In other words," Dr Godden said, "for the first time you've met someone else who has the same attitude toward you that you have. The attitude you think is the only thing you deserve."

She frowned at the rug. "Is that it?"

"Of course," he said. "But when you treated yourself that way, you always knew you had the choice, you could stop treating yourself that way whenever you wanted. But when this man Parker gives you the same treatment it's out of your control. He isn't even doing it to expiate your guilt. Your guilt has nothing to do with the way he acts."

"He doesn't care what I think," she said. "He doesn't *care*. Everybody cares. You might hate somebody, but you care what they think, you want to know what they think."

Dr Godden let the silence stretch this time, and she knew that meant she was supposed to look inside and see if there was anything else there, anything she was trying to hide from herself. "It isn't really Pam I'm angry about, is it?" she said.

"It isn't even me, not the real me."

"No?" he asked gently. "What is it, then?"

"The mask I'm wearing," she said. "Motherhood. You know, the good mother bit, the whole cop-out to make up for everything I've done wrong all my life. You know, how now I'm a mother and I hide behind that. And Parker doesn't pay any attention to the mask. He goes ahead and puts the guns in Pam's closet and doesn't even ask me. The whole mother mask doesn't mean a thing to him."

"You think he sees through it?"

"I think," she said, "I think he doesn't give a damn."

"What about Stan? Do you think he cares about Stan?"

"Parker? He doesn't care about anybody except his own sweet self."

Dr Godden said, "Then perhaps he'll arrange the robbery so he'll be the only one to get away."

"Do you think so?" she said, alarmed.

"I don't know. What do you think?"

She studied the question, trying to be fair, and finally said, "No, that isn't how he'd be. He's cold and ruthless and he doesn't care about anybody, but that's because he cares about *things*. Not even the money, I don't think. It's the plan that really matters to him. I think the thing that counts is doing it and having it come out right. So he wouldn't want anybody else to be caught."

"It would be unprofessional."

"Yes. Oh, they found a hideout."

"Did they?"

"Out Hilker Road. A hunting lodge up near the border that got burned down a couple of years ago."

"Andrews' Lodge?"

"I don't know, I guess so. They went up there yesterday to look it over."

"Then the plan is set?"

"Not entirely, I don't think. Maybe in Parker's mind it's all set, but they haven't talked about it all yet. I guess they're waiting for the others to come in."

"How many more?"

"Three. They're supposed to come in by Monday night, I think. So I guess I won't have much to tell you next time. But lots on Wednesday."

"That's when they'll be doing it." Dr Godden said.

Ellen shivered.

8

Jake Kengle unlocked his way into his furnished room, threw his briefcase on the bed, and got the bottle of whiskey out of the bottom dresser drawer. He went to the bathroom for a glass, half-filled it, and sat down on the bed to ease his feet while he slowly drank. The briefcase sat beside him, fat and black, sternly demanding he go back to work.

The hell with it. The double hell with it. He sipped at his whiskey, he looked moodily out the window at the airshaft with its gray brick wall five feet away, and he found some small pleasure in anticipating how good it was going to feel when he finally bent over and removed his shoes. His feet tingled inside the shoes, enjoying already their coming freedom. The liquor burned warm down his throat, slightly watering his eyes. The tension across his shoulders very gradually eased.

When he did at last bend forward to remove his shoes he saw out of the corner of his eye the briefcase again, still squatting there on the bed. In sudden rage he picked it up and hurled it across the room, generally in the direction of the window and the airshaft. His aim was way off; the briefcase hit the front of the dresser and thudded to the floor. Kengle left it there.

The briefcase contained something called a "presentation". A lot of brightly colored sheets of glossy paper, that meant; two expensive-looking loose-leaf folders, all telling how great some damn encyclopedia was.

Why would anybody buy an encyclopedia? Kengle didn't know. He'd been ringing doorbells day and night since

Tuesday on this damn job, and here it was Saturday afternoon, and he hadn't yet found anybody stupid enough to fork over three hundred bucks for a bunch of books. And the commission on zero sales is zero dollars.

It was a stinking way to make a buck, trying to sell things door-to-door on commission. But the good ways to make a buck, the soft and easy ways, they didn't show up all that often for the guy with a record. "In your employment résumé, Mr Kengle, you give no employer for the last fifty-two months. Why is that?"

"I was in prison."

"Oh? Mmmmmmmm."

He'd gotten out the first of September, and here it was the twenty-sixth already, and so far he'd landed two jobs, one peddling a food-freezer plan on commission and now this book thing. He'd been lucky the second day with the freezer plan, found a family that had just moved into this stinking town and had friends with a freezer plan, so they were what the boys called pre-sold. Sixty bucks commission. Then he'd gone the next ten days without a nibble, got into a stupid argument with Nettleton, the sales manager, and that was the end of that.

And how long is sixty bucks supposed to carry a guy? Monday they'd start bitching about the rent on this place, and he just didn't have it. So then what?

The trouble was, he wasn't a penny-ante boy. He could hustle into a big-time caper, cut ten or twenty thousand for himself, handle his action with no trouble. But cop some old lady's purse in the park for six dollars and thirty-seven cents? He'd never done it, he had no taste for it, and it seemed to him an ignominious thing to get the collar for. So it looked as though he was going to sit here in this room — or out in the street, if they threw him out of the room — and starve, because he couldn't turn an honest dollar and wouldn't turn a dishonest nickel.

The briefcase lay on the floor like a legless bug on its back. The sales manager — Smith, this one's name was, and as phony a bastard as Nettleton — had told him the weekend was always a hot time for book sales, because of husbands and kids being home. Well, it had been crap so far today, and here it was three in the afternoon. So should he go fight it some more? Who the hell works on Saturday afternoon? Or Saturday evening, or all day Sunday? Ex-cons trying to make a commission buck, that's who.

If that bastard lawyer hadn't used up every penny of his stake in useless appeals things wouldn't be so bad now. He could sit back, relax, live small but comfortable until somebody showed up with something. But no. He had to hustle books like some baggy-pants straight man in burlesque.

He finished the liquor in the glass, got to his feet and padded in his socks over to the dresser. He was reaching for the bottle when somebody knocked on the door.

Weren't they going to wait till Monday? All set to blow his top, Kengle went over and opened the door, and there stood a tall skinny kid in an undershirt. "Phone for you," he said, and trotted away down the hall.

This was a sweet place. One telephone on each floor, in the hall near the elevator, and a pay phone at that. When it rang it was up to anybody who heard it to go answer it and pass the word to whoever it was for. That was the kind of privacy Kengle loved.

Kengle locked his door and walked down the hall to the phone. Maybe it was Smith, checking to see if he was out hustling those books. If so, screw Smith.

The voice said, "Jake?"

Kengle recognized it, and a heavy weight seemed to lift off his back. The voice belonged to Ed Dant, who ran a fleabag hotel in Atlanta and who was Kengle's permanent address. Anybody in the business who wanted to contact him knew to call Ed Dant, who did the same thing for half a dozen other guys. When he'd moved into this place here Kengle had telegraphed Ed the address and phone number right away, because when the break came it would be coming through a call from Ed.

Keeping all trace of excitement out of his voice, Kengle said, "What's new, pal?"

"Nothing much. Just to say hello, glad to hear you're out, see how you're doing."

"Fine. Got a steady job."

"Glad to hear it. Ran into an old friend of yours the other day. Remember Marty Fusco?"

"Sure. How's he doing these days?"

"Working here and there. He thought he might drop by and see you tomorrow. I wasn't sure I had the address right, so I told him I'd call him back."

Kengle reeled off his address.

They talked a little more, saying nothing, and then ended the conversation. Kengle was grinning from ear to ear when he walked back down the hall and unlocked his way into his room.

One corner of his brain said, *What if the set-up's no good?*

Aloud he said, "It's gotta be better than peddling books."

He made one concession to good sense. He opened the window before throwing the briefcase into the airshaft.

9

"MAYBE I ought to tell the police," Ellen said. She was hugging herself so hard her arms hurt.

"I don't think you should," Dr Godden said carefully. "I think you're carrying around enough guilt feelings as it is."

"It's tonight," she said. She was shivering, trembling, no matter how hard she hugged herself.

"If Stan had had his way," Dr Godden reminded her, "it would have been happening right now."

"Nobody has their way against Parker," she said. "I hate him."

"I believe we correctly analyzed Stan on Monday," Dr Godden said. "He wanted a daylight robbery so that he could not be asked to take an active part in it."

"If I told the police it was going to happen," she said, "but didn't tell them who was going to do it, and then somehow I let Stan know they knew about it—"

"You couldn't do it," he told her. "Not without implicating yourself. And then Stan would merely hate you."

"But there's no way out! If they get caught, *that's* terrible, and if they don't get caught he'll want to do it again and *that's* terrible."

"We still can't be sure he'll want to do it again," Dr Godden said, his voice soothing her though she still trembled. "After all, if he didn't want to take an active part this time it means he's had some second thoughts already, he's somewhat afraid now. After the reality of the experience he may decide he never wants to go through anything like that again. We can't tell one way or the other until he's actually gone through it."

"But what if they get caught?"

"Let's go over the plan," he said, "and see if we can find any loopholes, anything Parker and the others haven't thought of. We've discussed various parts of the plan from time to time, but we've never taken it through from beginning to end. Let's do that now."

"All right," she said. Her voice began to drone.

10

DR GODDEN stood in the doorway, watched Ellen Fusco go out through the outer office, and then motioned to the slender young man on the Naugahyde sofa to come in.

The young man, whose face was covered with acne, got to his feet, said nastily, "Ralph's late again," and sauntered into the inner office. He sat on the sofa there, spread his legs out, folded his arms and said, "Ralph's always late."

Dr Godden shut the door, controlled his impulse to speak harshly, and went over to sit in his accustomed chair at the end of the sofa. "That's a problem of Ralph's," he said. "Perhaps after a while he'll get over it."

"Soon everyone will be perfect," said the young man. He always strove for sarcasm but never attained anything other than petulance.

His name was Roger St Cloud, he was twenty-two years old, militarily unsuitable because of some problem with his inner ear, the only son of well-to-do parents — his father had a controlling interest in Monequois First Savings — and a classic bundle of insecurities and neuroses masked by a juvenile nastiness of manner. The clothing he wore — sneakers without socks, filthy chinos, a ratty turtleneck sweater — was intended to infuriate his parents, and it succeeded. It was the positive relish with which Roger's parents rose to every bait the boy tossed them that made Dr Godden's work so much more necessary and at the same time so much more difficult. If he could get the parents in here for regular treatments it might have some good effect on the son, but of course they'd never agree to anything like that.

Well, for the purpose at hand what was needed was not the parents but the son. Dr Godden said, out of the sense of duty that had been troubling him of late, "While we wait for Ralph, is there anything you'd like to talk about?"

Roger shrugged carelessly, which always meant yes, always meant there was something he felt about so strongly that the feeling embarrassed him and therefore had to be denied. "Had another dream," he said.

"The Dragon?" That was the dream about his mother.

"No, none of the usual. A new one."

"Ah? What was it?"

"I was walking down a rifle barrel. It was like a tunnel, you know? But it was a rifle barrel, and I was walking toward the bullets. I could look back the other way and see daylight at the hole. It was very realistic, with the shiny metal color and everything. It was cold in there. Then I looked back and there was an eye down at the far end looking at me. It was my father, and he said, 'You'll never get away.' But he was big, he was normal size for the rifle, so he couldn't get at me. But he kept looking in, his eye there, and I shouted, 'Get out of the way! You'll be killed when the gun goes off!' But he wouldn't believe me. Then there was a boom, like an explosion. Not like a rifle shot at all. A real explosion. And I looked and there was a bullet coming toward me. It looked like a train in a tunnel, except it filled it all the way around, there wasn't any place to squeeze in and let it go by. And the front was all fat and squashed. I started running away, but I was slow, it turned slow-motion, you know, the way they do. But the bullet was slow, too, it was just behind me but it couldn't catch up. And my father's eye was still up at the other end, he wouldn't get out of the way. I kept hollering at him, but he wouldn't get out of the way."

In the course of telling all this, Roger's voice had lost its usual whine, his expression had calmed, and he had shown briefly who it was he might have been if things had been different. But now his face twisted back into its usual expression, the whine came into his voice again, and he shrugged negligently, saying, "That's when I woke up."

"Not hard to interpret, that dream," Dr Godden suggested.

"Easy. I'm afraid of getting caught and I'm afraid of getting killed."

"And you're also afraid that if you do get caught your disgrace will also ruin your father."

Roger shrugged.

The door burst open and Ralph lumbered in. A tall, heavyset, very strong man of thirty-two, he gave an appearance of flabbiness and weakness that was totally misleading. His strength was hampered by clumsiness, his appearance altered by the way he stooped and shambled, but within the self-negating mannerisms was a strong and capable body waiting to be unleashed.

"I ran," Ralph said, panting, and thudded over to drop heavily onto the sofa beside Roger.

"You *always* run," Roger commented.

Ralph never took offence at Roger's comments. Why should he, when he believed he deserved them? Ralph believed that he was stupid, and that stupidity was a crime. Any asset he might have, such as a strong body or a handsome face, had to be denied because it would be improper for him to enjoy anything while still committing the crime of stupidity. What had driven Ralph to Dr Godden was a girl friend who had made it a condition of their continued relationship, but what had driven him to the set of mind that he lived by Dr Godden hadn't as yet been able to learn. It was somewhere in the early years, and Ralph's blankness on that period was itself a strong indication that Dr Godden was on the right track.

Now, Ralph's reply to Roger was only a sheepish grinning, "I'm always late." Then he sat there and panted.

Dr Godden looked at them, his assistants, and he found himself envying the man Ellen knew as Parker. When Parker made a plan he knew the parts of it would be carried out by professionals, solid reliable men who did this sort of thing for a living. Dr Godden would have preferred to work with professionals himself, but according to Ellen these people did have loyalty among themselves and in the normal way of things wouldn't steal from one another. Honor among thieves apparently did exist after all.

So it was Roger and Ralph. Dr Godden had gone through the list of his patients, had sounded a few of them out very gently and obliquely, and it had come down at last to Roger and Ralph.

Roger had been easy to convince; perhaps, from the sound of last night's dream, he'd been too easy. But if Roger had any hidden doubts or apprehensions, Dr Godden prided himself he'd be able to contain them at least until the night's work was over. Ralph, burly and cumbersome and self-doubting, had taken longer to persuade, but in the end his trust for Dr Godden had swung it, and now he was committed without question.

The same basic argument had been used on both of them; it would be therapy. To Ralph: "Here's a chance to prove you are capable after all. With this accomplishment behind you, there's no telling how much we'll be able to unlock, how much more of you we'll be able to free." And to Roger: "You'll never find a better opportunity to express all your independence and revolt at once. Do this, act out all your aggressions and resentments in this one action, do it successfully, and you'll be well on your way to the independence we both know you need for self-fulfillment."

Dr Godden's own reasons were more mundane; he needed money. With a rapacious ex-wife bleeding him white for alimony and child support payments, with a second wife who didn't know the meaning of the word economy, and with Mary Beth — a patient now become mistress — becoming more expensive every month, Dr Godden had been teetering at the brink of financial chaos for over a year now. And to top it off this man Nolan had reappeared, demanding money to keep his mouth shut, threatening to open up that business in New York again, to let the local medical society know his credentials weren't entirely in order.

Fred Godden never intended to get into trouble or to break the law, things just happened around him. Like California, where he'd started out and where the brother-in-law of a patient had gotten him involved in that abortion business. He himself had performed no abortions, he'd only served as a middleman, but when that one girl died the investigation dragged in a lot of wriggling fish, Dr Fred Godden among them. The authorities had never quite accepted the idea that the dead girl — and three others they'd found — had all coincidentally come to him as psychiatric patients shortly before their abortions, but they hadn't been able to prove anything. Still, it had seemed wisest to leave California, particularly since his first wife had chosen the blow-up as an excuse to divorce him, just as though it hadn't been her free-spending that had driven him into the racket in the first place.

In New York he had developed a new practice and a new wife, but his taste in women seemed doomed not to change, and wife number two spent just as frantically as had wife number one, so when one of his patients came up with the drug suggestion he was ready for it.

How did they know, that's what bothered him, how did these people always know he'd be open to their suggestions, weak enough to agree, to lend his respectable façade to their schemes. He'd studied his face in the bathroom mirror more than once, and as far as he could see he didn't *look* shady. And he'd heard tape recordings of his voice; and he didn't *sound* shady. So how did they know?

They knew, that's all. As a doctor, he could get hold of drugs, especially the new chemicals, the psychedelics. As a doctor specializing in psychoanalysis, his cover was perfect for the people who needed someone to act as a source of supply and a base for distribution. And if one of the shuffling bearded oddballs who'd come to him for the yellow capsules hadn't turned out to be a policeman, one of the New York City Police Department undercover narcotics men, he might still be there, in New York City, with the lucrative practice and the even more lucrative sideline, instead of here in this sinkhole.

He'd gotten out of it in New York, too, though he'd spent nine days in jail, in the Tombs, and had come out of it stripped of his credentials and legal permission to operate either as a doctor or an analyst. But how else could he made a living? That was why he'd moved up to this godforsaken area, where a man's bona fides were unlikely to be very closely scrutinized, but where the number of patients – and their ability to pay – was depressingly low.

And then Nolan had showed up. One of the buyers back in New York, Nolan had known everything about Dr Godden's connection with the gang, and now here he was in Monequois, demanding money as the price of his silence. How Nolan had found him Dr Godden didn't know, any more than he had known at first where he could possibly find the money to pay him.

But hard on the heels of Nolan had come the sudden revelation from Ellen Fusco, and all at once it had seemed to Dr Godden that there was a way out after all, that he could see daylight at the end of the tunnel.

What he would do after tonight he himself wasn't entirely sure. Would he merely pay off Nolan and all his outstanding debts, then tuck the rest away for the next crisis? Or would he pack his bags and leave the whole mess, start again somewhere else under another name, leave wives and children and mistresses and blackmailer and all? If that was what he wanted, there'd be money enough. Ralph and Roger, not having been told the true scope of the affair, were content to be receiving ten thousand dollars each. That meant almost the whole thing for Dr Godden, estimated by Ellen Fusco at four hundred thousand dollars.

Four hundred thousand dollars. To tackle people like Parker and Fusco and Devers and the others Ellen had told him about, to risk the precarious balance he now had, to take a chance on using these two poor incompetents, it was all worth it for four hundred thousand dollars.

He had thought about it often. He well knew the danger in seeking the Holy Grail, he'd seen it frequently enough in his patients. "If only X happens, everything will be all right." The belief in the easy one-shot panacea more frequently led to disaster than salvation.

So he couldn't allow himself to think of it in all-encompassing terms. Even with the four hundred thousand in his hands, he would still be Fred Godden, Dr Fred Godden, with a shady past and a penny-ante practice, with a wife and an ex-wife and a mistress and a certain bleak awareness of his own tendency toward erratic behaviour when it came to women, and with a history of bad errors of judgement leading him into trouble. Nothing would change after tonight except his financial status. He would be wealthy, but he would still be the same man.

Knowing that, being sure not to forget it, he had studied the proposition, the possibilities, the dangers, the rewards, and at last he had made up his mind. An opportunity like this wouldn't be coming his way twice. He'd be a fool to let this one slip by.

Tonight.

Dr Godden looked at Roger and Ralph. His mob. They would have to do.

He took a deep breath, "I taped Mrs Fusco's session just now," he said. "She's given us their plans from beginning to end. We'll listen to them first, and then go over our own plans once more."

Ralph and Roger looked alert, Dr Godden pressed the switch and the voice of Ellen Fusco, faintly metallic, began once more to drone.

Part Three

1

THE PHONE rang. Parker awoke at once, put the receiver to his ear, and the operator said, "Eleven o'clock, Mr Lynch."

"Thank you." It was Wednesday. The heist was tonight.

Parker got out of bed and padded nude to the bathroom. He showered and shaved, then dressed in black rubber-soled oxford shoes, black trousers, white shirt open at the collar. He left the room, locked it after him, and went across the highway to the diner where he'd had breakfast every day of his stay here. He knew now what was safe to order and what was not.

The waitress knew him, too. She came over smiling when he sat down, saying, "Good morning, Mr Lynch. Getting a late start this morning."

"Leaving today," he said. He would have preferred a waitress who minded her own business, but this was a cheery gregarious stocky woman and there was nothing to be done about it. Rather than have her remember him specifically as the customer who'd been surly to her, he'd maintained a small conversation with her every day, allowing himself to be just another salesman passing through, spending a couple of weeks at the motel across the way. He would be much less specific in her mind then, and if the law did come around in a day or two her description of him would be that much more vague.

Now, "Sorry to lose you," she said. "What'll it be this morning?"

He ordered scrambled eggs, bacon, orange juice, black coffee, then sat and looked out the window at the trucks going by on the highway. He ate his food when it came, left an ordinary tip, paid the cashier at the door, and walked back across the road to the motel.

He went into the motel office and the woman at the desk looked at him brightly. "Yes, sir?"

"I'm checking out."

"Yes, sir. What room number, please?"

"Eleven."

"Do you have your key?"

"I'll leave it in the room. My luggage is still there."

"Very good."

She opened a file drawer and got out his bill. "Any charges this morning? Phone calls, anything like that?"

"No."

"Very good."

She slid the bill across the counter to him. One hundred forty dollars. He took out his wallet, began to slide some of Norman Berridge's bills on to the desk.

"Cash?" she said in surprise.

This was a bad moment, and he knew it, but there was no way around it. To skip out on the bill would have the cops looking for him a day early. Have them looking for Devers' Pontiac, which had been here often enough to be known in the last three weeks. But he couldn't carry credit cards or a checkbook, at least not legitimately, and it was bad business to kite checks in the neighbourhood of a score. Got the law on your trail too soon and too easy. So he was going to have to pay this motel bill, and the only way to do it was with cash.

He shrugged at the woman's surprise, therefore, and said, "That's what the company accountant says we have to do from now on. It's something to do with taxes. I liked it better the old way. Hand over an American Express card and that's it."

"You'll want a receipt," she said.

"It's the only way I get reimbursed," he said.

She stamped the bill paid, gave it to him, and scooped the bills off the desk. "Thank you for staying with us, sir. Do come again."

Parker went back outside. It was a good day, sunny but with a bite in the air. He walked down the row to his unit and unlocked the door. The cleaning girl's cart was two doors farther along. He went inside, left the door open, and packed his one suitcase, leaving out only a long-sleeve high-neck black pullover sweater, a dark gray sport jacket and a quiet blue-and-black tie. He put the tie in the side pocket of the sport jacket, set the closed suitcase on the floor and lay down on the bed with his eyes closed to wait.

He sensed when the light changed, meaning there was someone standing in the doorway. He opened his eyes and it was the cleaning girl. "I'll be out of here by twelve-thirty," he said, and she went away.

It was quarter past twelve when he heard the tires grate on gravel in front of his room. He sat up, saw the Pontiac coming to a stop out there, and got off the bed again.

It was Devers, on his lunch hour. He got out of the car as Parker stepped out into the sunlight, carrying his suitcase in his right hand, his sport jacket and sweater in his left.

Devers said, "You want to drive?"

"Why?"

Devers laughed and shook his head. "I'll tell you the truth, it's because I'm a nervous wreck. I'm really shaky today."

Parker nodded. "I'll drive," he said. He put his gear in the back seat and got behind the wheel as Devers trotted around and came in on the passenger side.

Devers had left the engine running. Parker put it in reverse, backed it around in a tight half-circle, switched into drive and joined the thin stream of westbound traffic on the highway.

Devers said, "You get used to it after a while?"

"After a while," Parker agreed. "Some guys always get flutters before. Some always get them after."

"When do you get yours?"

"I don't."

He wasn't boasting, it was the truth. The situation they were going into tonight would only make him colder and colder, harder and harder, surer and surer. He knew everything was organized, he knew the way it was supposed to come off, the step-by-step working out of the prepared script, and he was like a cold-blooded stage manager on opening night; no jitters, just a hard determination that everything would happen the way it was supposed to happen. He knew that the others, the actors, were all atremble, but that wasn't for him. Stage managers don't tremble.

Not even when something goes wrong. That was what he was there for tonight, just as much as his pre-planned actions. He was there also to be ready for the unexpected, to improvise if anything went wrong, to keep the production safe and moving no matter what. So he couldn't get the flutters before or during, and it didn't make any sense to get them after. So he just didn't get the flutters.

Devers wiped his mouth with the back of his hand. "Boy, I don't know," he said. "I don't know how you go about getting used to something like this."

"You keep doing it," Parker told him.

"Yeah, I guess so."

Just this side of North Bangor there was a white clapboard house with a sign hanging from a tree out front reading: TOURISTS. Behind the house were half a dozen cabins, miniature versions of the house. A black Buick station wagon was parked next to one of the cabins. Devers gestured a thumb at it as they drove by, saying, "They haven't left yet."

"They'll be along," Parker said.

"They" were the other three men, Jake Kengle and Philly Webb and Bill Stockton, all of whom had come into town on Monday, had listened to the outline of the caper, and had elected to be dealt in. The station wagon was Webb's, and the only constant about it was its brand; it never stopped being a Buick. But it hadn't been black more than a week or two, and would be some color other than black by the end of this week. And the Maryland license plates it sported now were only one of the many sets it had known in the past and would know in the future. Webb prided himself out loud on having attained the untraceable car, but Parker thought it likelier that Webb just liked to have something to play with.

He took the right turn before Monequois that bypassed the town and went directly out to the air base. He stopped before the main gate and Devers said, "See you tonight."

"Right."

Devers climbed out and walked away toward the gate. Parker turned the car toward Monequois.

He reached the Fusco house at one o'clock, and put the car in place beside the house. The day was beginning to warm up a little, but it wouldn't get much above seventy before starting back down again two or three hours from now.

Parker went into the house. Fusco was seated at the kitchen table, eating a bowl of cereal. He called, "I'm baby-sitting. Ellen's off to see her shrink. Said she'll be back a little after two."

Parker didn't care where she was or when she'd be back. He said, "Did you get the coats?"

"In the bedroom closet."

"Good."

Parker left the living-room and went down the short hall to the master bedroom. It was neat and plain and functional and impersonal, like the rest of the house. It was Ellen Fusco's room, and either she or he had managed to create a room that gave no sign of occupancy at all. The dresser top was bare, there was no clothing on the chair beside the bed, the nightstands held neat metallic lamps and clean ashtrays, the bed was anonymously and neatly made.

There were two closets. The one Parker opened first was full of the woman's clothing, neat and rigid. The other one was Devers', and it seemed sloppy by comparison, even though the clothing was all on hangers. But the shoes on the floor were not lined up in pairs, and the shelf was cluttered with stray objects.

In Devers' closet were the coats. Tunics, really, like the white pullover tunics worn by some barbers and dentists. But these weren't white, they were glistening metallic gold, as bright as the gold foil around a chocolate candy, seeming to glitter and sparkle inside the closet with their own light. They had long sleeves, high hard collars and elastic wrists. They looked as though they should be worn by a team of Cossack acrobats on television.

Parker took one of the tunics out, looked at it in the light, nodded in satisfaction and put it back again. It had been worth Fusco's trip to New York City, to a costume rental place there. These tunics had the right look to them.

He went back to the living-room. In the kitchen, Fusco was now rinsing out his cereal bowl. Parker called to him, "They look good."

Fusco shut the water off. "You like them? I had to try three places." He dried his hands on a dishtowel and came into the living room. "You should see what they tried to give me."

Parker sat down on the sofa. "You got everything of yours cleaned out of here?"

"Sure," Fusco said. "There wasn't that much. I sent off a package Railway Express this morning." He'd checked out of his hotel Sunday morning, had been sleeping on the sofa here since then, except for last night when he'd slept at a hotel in New York.

"To an address?" Parker asked him.

"To Manhattan. To be picked up."

"Good."

"You want coffee? Something to drink?"

"Nothing."

Parker shut his eyes. He knew most people tended to get jumpy the day of a score, knew that jumpy people like to talk. He didn't want to be talked to, and the easiest way to avoid it was by keeping his eyes shut. People leave you alone if you have your eyes shut, even if they know you're awake.

He sat there like that, waiting, not thinking about much of anything, giving stray thoughts to Puerto Rico and Claire, until Fusco said, "Here's the boys." Then he opened his eyes and got to his feet.

The station wagon was parked out front. Three men were walking toward the house, Jake Kengle in the lead. Behind him was Bill Stockton, a tall skinny guy with black hair and a loose-limbed, stooped way of walking. Bringing up the rear was Philly Webb, who owned the station wagon and who would be driving tonight. He was short, chunky, olive-complexioned, with the chest and arms of a weightlifter, giving him a vaguely apelike look.

Fusco opened the door for them and they trooped in, all dressed like Parker in white shirts, black trousers and quiet-soled shoes. Kengle said, "This is the part I don't like. Just before, you know? When there's nothing to do but wait."

"There might be a deck of cards around here," said Webb.

"Sure," said Fusco. "We can play at the kitchen table. I'll be right back."

Parker sat out, but the other four worked up a poker game to kill the time, most draw and five-card stud. They played for small stakes; it was a superstition that it was bad luck to gamble with money you hadn't copped yet.

Parker didn't gamble. He preferred to sit in the living-room, either doing nothing at all or going over again in his mind each step of what they were supposed to do today, trying to find things that had been overlooked.

Ellen came back about twenty after two. She looked at the four sitting around the kitchen table, and said to Parker, "How much longer are you all going to be here?"

"A little while," he told her.

She was acting like somebody being calm with a great deal of trouble. She fluttered a bit in the living-room, and then went on out to the bedroom. Parker watched her go, frowning. He didn't like the way she was acting, hadn't liked any of the changes she'd gone through the last week and a half.

It had started with that oddball stupid sexless proposition. It had been a proposition, it couldn't have been anything else, but it had been delivered in such a way as to make it tough to believe it had ever happened. As though she'd done it against her will, and had just gone through the motions without really meaning it.

But she'd meant it, he was sure of that. She'd spent a couple of days giving him cow eyes alternating with bad temper as though he'd been the one trying to put the make on her, and then it had been all over, with a new phase coming in.

The new phase had been hatred, cold silent murderous hatred. Whenever he'd been in the house she was always somewhere around, glaring at him, as though waiting for him to make the one move that would make it all right for her to come after him with a carving knife.

But that hadn't lasted either. It seemed as though every time she went off for one of her sessions with the analyst she came back with a different set on the world. The next attitude toward Parker had been studied indifference; she'd ignored him as completely as if he weren't there at all. But not arrogantly, not like a queen ignoring a peasant, which is ignoring in a way that still acknowledges existence. Parker seemed to have ceased to exist for her, as though she had a blind spot and he was standing in the middle of it.

That phase had been the easiest to put up with, but it too had changed, and the most recent attitude had been fear, a kind of guilty jumpy fear that had made him almost as nervous in her presence as she was. He'd asked both Devers and Fusco about it, and they'd both assured him she would have done nothing — like talking to the law — to justify her guilt or her fear. "That's just the way she gets sometimes," Devers had said. Fusco's comment had been, "Ellen wouldn't fink, period." Parker had had to take their word for it, but he still didn't like it; when she slunk and jumped and jittered around him like that it made his hackles rise.

Well, this was the end of it anyway. He'd be leaving this house for the last time this afternoon, and Ellen Fusco could stumble on through life without him.

But there was one last session with her to be gone through. A little after three she came back into the living-room and sat down on the other end of the sofa. She was smoking, and she kept nervously tapping the cigarette on an ashtray.

She was going to say something, but she was taking her time. Parker waited, and finally she said, not looking at him, "What if something goes wrong?"

He turned his head and looked at her. She was studying the ashtray on the coffee table, tapping and tapping the cigarette against it. He said, "Like what?"

She made a convulsive shrugging movement. "I don't know. Anything. The alarm goes out too soon. Somebody asks for identification at the wrong time. Anything at all."

"We handle it, if we can," he said.

"But it could happen."

"It can always happen."

"Maybe it's the wrong kind of job," she said.

He looked at her, waiting for her to go on. She sat there, tap-tapping, huddled in on herself, clasping her left upper arm with her right hand as though to hug herself, and although the fear of him seemed to be gone now — another change — the nervousness was even worse than before. She was like an old car with an engine that's falling apart; you can just see the hood vibrating, but underneath there it's throwing a rod.

When he kept on being silent, not responding to her comment about the wrong kind of job, she tossed him a quick look — her eyes were large and round and panic-stricken — stared back at the ashtray, and said, "Oh, not for you, maybe. Maybe you like this kind of thing. But maybe it's wrong for Stan. Or even Marty. But mostly Stan."

"It's his choice," Parker said.

"I wish he wasn't involved."

"Talk to him."

"I did. A long time ago. The point is—" She stopped, shook her head, frowned at her cigarette, all as though she wasn't entirely sure what the point was. Finally she said, "The point is, what happens to Stan if something goes wrong? He isn't a professional, maybe he won't be able to get away. And it would matter to him, don't you see? Marty, it doesn't matter to Marty, he goes to jail, he comes back out, he does the exact same thing again. Jake Kengle was in jail, too, it's the same thing. But Stan isn't like that. It would matter to him, if he was in jail."

Parker wondered how she could believe there was anyone

on earth to whom a jail term didn't matter. But what he said was, "Maybe Stan thinks he won't go to jail."

"I know. It's worth the risk, everybody's sure it's worth the risk."

"Maybe it is."

"Why don't you—?"

She stopped again, shook her head violently, finally took a drag on the cigarette. With one last tap at the ashtray, she rose in a cloud of expelled smoke.

Parker said, "Why don't we what?"

"Nothing," she said, turning away.

"Why don't we call it off?"

She shook her head and walked out of the living-room. He knew that's what she'd been about to say, that while starting to say it the impossibility of it all had come through to her — the costumes were in the closet, the guns in the kid's room, the bus out at the lodge, the string assembled and playing poker in the next room — and she'd stopped herself before saying the whole thing. But it was what she wanted, that much was obvious. To have it not happen, never be going to happen.

It wasn't the first time Parker had seen somebody's woman get that kind of last-minute jitters, and it probably wouldn't be the last. It was good to have a woman like Claire, strong enough and secure enough and smart enough to stay out of it entirely. It would be good to get back to San Juan, to see Claire again, to relax beside the ocean, to spend some time in the casino.

Parker didn't go to the casino for himself, but for Claire. She did the gambling, if it could be called that.

The casinos in San Juan didn't have the desperate greedy urgency of Las Vegas, where the gambling rooms have neither clocks nor windows to remind the fish of the passing of time. In San Juan the casinos were merely entertainment appendages of the tourist industry, along with the beaches and the floor shows and the boat rides to St Thomas for duty-free liquor. The hotel casinos were only open eight hours a day, from eight in the evening till four in the morning, and only three kinds of gambling were available for the idle speculator: roulette, blackjack, craps.

Claire's specialty was craps. She invariably, upon entering the casino, bought fifty one-dollar chips and headed for whichever crap table was the least crowded. There she would spend her fifty chips one at a time, exclusively on side bets, always passing the dice when they came around to her, and winning about one time in three. She was the most passive of gamblers, but the action exhilarated her, so that as the stack of fifty dwindled slowly away her eyes always got brighter, her movements more electric, her expressions more excited. Every time, she would turn away from the table after the loss of the final chip as vibrant and exuberant as if she'd just broken the bank. Gambling was like a good alcohol high with her, it made her enjoy life more, enjoy herself more. Afterward, they always went from the casino straight back to the hotel and to bed, where she would be at her most inventive and eager.

Yes. It would be good to get back to San Juan, good to see Claire again.

It surprised him a little that his thoughts were becoming sexual. That was another change Claire was making in him. The way it used to be, sex was always an urgent, vital, all-consuming thing with him right after a heist, slowly then tapering off until he had no interest along that line at all, and that's when he would be ready for another job. But now, because of Claire, it was different. Here he was, the day of the heist itself, his mind full of pictures of Claire on white sheets in the semi-dark air-conditioned room in San Juan, the sun bright outside the windows, all the tourists and natives hustling in the outside world while Claire's arms reached up and folded around him.

He sat there in the living room and let his mind drift wherever it wanted to go until his watch read four o'clock. Then he got to his feet and went out to the kitchen and said, "Time to go."

"Right," said Webb. He was out of the hand being played, so he got to his feet, took his handful of bills from the table and tucked them away in a pocket, and yawned and stretched, his arms seeming grotesquely long for his stubby body when he spread them out.

The other three finished the hand, which Kengle won with jacks over threes.

Raking in the pot, Kengle grinned and said, "Looks like my luck's changing. It's about time."

Stockton said, "Mine better change before tonight."

"How'd you do?" Fusco asked Kengle.

"Made about eighteen."

"I'm ahead three," Webb said.

"I took a bath," Stockton said, getting to his feet.

Fusco said, "Parker, I'll be with you in a minute. I've got to say so long to Ellen."

"Bring the costumes out with you."

"Right."

Stockton said, "Where's the armament?"

"This way."

Stockton and Kengle followed Parker down the hall to the kid's bedroom. She was in bed now for her afternoon nap, all wrapped up in a filthy blanket she carried around with her all the time. Parker opened the closet door and handed out the cartons to the other two, who took them and tiptoed out of the room. Parker shut the door of the closet and followed them.

Fusco was still in the bedroom with Ellen. Kengle, his arms full of boxes claiming to contain road-racer sets, stood in the middle of the living-room and gestured toward the bedroom with his head, saying, "Marty getting a little off the ex-wife?"

"No," Parker said. "He's just being a good guest, thanking her for all the breakfasts."

Kengle made a face and nodded. "That sounds like Marty," he said. "You should of seen him in stir. Polite to the screws."

Webb, his hand on the doorknob, said, "We'll see you out there, Parker."

"Right."

The three went out, Webb leading the way and the other two carrying the cartons. They were put in the back of the station wagon and a minute later the wagon pulled away.

Parker stood by the open door, waiting. It was three or four minutes before Fusco came out, holding the tunics up by their hangers, a worried expression on his face. "Boy, Parker," he said. "She's really nervous. I guess me taking a fall really shook her up."

"She'll survive," Parker said. "You want to put those things in a bag or something. Somebody'll see us going out with those things."

"Nobody pays any attention in a neighborhood like this," Fusco said. "Nobody's looked at either of us any time we came in or out here."

"That's because they can figure us, even if they're wrong. Ellen's a divorcée, we're men. But those are crazy gold pajama tops, and people'll remember them. We don't want the law around here tomorrow, asking Ellen where'd the guys go with the gold pajama tops."

"And the gold. Okay, you're right. Just a minute."

Fusco got a brown paper bag from the kitchen, took the tunics off their hangers, rolled them one at a time and stuffed them into the bag. When he was done, he and Parker went out to the Pontiac. Parker's suitcase and sweater and sport jacket were still on the back seat, and Fusco now added the bag of tunics to them. Parker got behind the wheel.

They drove east out of Monequois, past the air base, and left up Hiker Road. They went past the South Gate and continued on northward another four miles, until they came to a dirt road leading uphill away to the left. They took this and Parker shifted into low. The road climbed steeply, with sharp curves. Never anything more than a track beaten into and scraped out of the mountainside by a bulldozer, it had now been out of use for three years and showed it. Deep meandering grooves showed where the runoff from mountain rains was making paths for itself toward the valley. Here and there tree branches hung low, scraping the roof of the car, and in two spots thick fallen branches lay beside the road where Parker and Devers and Fusco had shoved them out of the way the first time they'd driven up here.

It was three miles, almost all uphill, all on minimal road, until at last they came to the burned-out lodge. It had been a large building, two storeys high, of stone and log, and it had been almost entirely gutted by fire. A garage behind it, originally large enough for a dozen cars, had been partially burned away, with now only one end of it still intact, enough for three cars. Another out-building, a large workshed, hadn't been touched at all.

Of the original building only the stone walls were left, extending from three to seven feet up at different spots around the perimeter. Inside these walls was a jumble of black lines, the charred remains of beams and walls, made anonymous and smooth by three summers and winters. Grass was growing here and there inside, little areas of green.

Half a dozen "No Trespassing" signs had been fixed to trees or the remaining stone walls, but there was no sign anyone had been around recently to see if the signs were being obeyed. The garage and workshed were both stripped and bare, and it was obvious no one was in any hurry to rebuild Andrews' Lodge. It looked, in fact, suspiciously like the result of somebody's having burned his business down for the insurance, which doesn't happen when the business is showing a steady profit. Andrews' Lodge had probably been losing a lot of its business to Canadian hunting areas, which hadn't been as extensively hunted, so that game was still plentiful.

The station wagon was nowhere in sight, but when Parker drove the Pontiac around the corner of the lodge shell Stockton was standing beside an open garage door in the unburned end of the garage, motioning at them to come on. In this setting he looked like a modern-day Ichabod Crane, tall and skinny and stoop-shouldered.

Parker drove the car into the garage and cut the engine as Stockton shut the two doors. He and Fusco got out of the Pontiac, and Parker got his sport jacket and sweater from the back seat.

There were no interior walls separating the garage stalls. The Pontiac was the nearest to the burned portion, and next to it on the other side was the Buick station wagon. At the far end was the bus.

It was a small bus, shorter than usual, the kind of thing frequently used by small private schools to transport their children. It had been that yellow color when Parker had first seen it at the junkyard in Baltimore, but a lot had been done to it since then. It had a different color now, a rich royal blue that looked dark inside the garage here but would look as bright as a swimming pool out in the sunlight. It also had a different engine, much hotter than the original plant it had had under its hood. The false set of Maryland plates that had brought it up here were in the process of being changed now by Webb to New York plates which were equally false but for which they had faked-up registration. Kengle was in the process of attaching to the near side one of the two cloth banners they'd made, in red letters on white, reading:

ERNIE SEVEN AND THE FOUR SCORE

This was where most of Norman Berridge's money had gone, into this bus and the musical instruments showing conspicuously through the rear windows.

Parker walked around the Buick and stood looking at the banner for a minute. Kengle grinned at him, saying, "Looks good, don't it?"

"Just so it looks real," Parker said.

"Then that's what it looks," Kengle said. "It looks real."

Parker agreed with him. A bus that made itself as conspicuous as this had to lull suspicions.

Parker carried his sweater and sport jacket into the bus and dropped them on a seat toward the rear. Fusco had followed him aboard, and when he turned round he saw Fusco getting the gold tunics out of the brown paper bag, shaking them out one at a time, smoothing out the wrinkles, and draping each across the back of a bus seat.

Parker edged by Fusco and stepped down out of the bus again. Kengle was now around on the other side, putting the second banner there. A third, smaller but just as bright, was being put on the back by Stockton. Webb, having replaced both licence plates, was putting his tools away in the kit in the back of his station wagon.

They were ready to go at ten to five. They all got aboard the bus except Stockton, who opened the garage doors. The doors had been padlocked shut, but Parker and Fusco had sawn through the padlocks so they could be removed and then replaced to look as though they were still secure.

Those in the bus slipped on their tunics and settled in seats, all toward the front. Webb got behind the wheel, started the engine, which sounded deceptively ordinary, and backed the bus out into tree-dappled sunlight. Stockton shut the garage doors and replaced the padlock while Webb turned the bus around, then came over and climbed aboard, but didn't put his tunic on yet.

The trip down the dirt road was painfully slow, Webb being careful not to rattle the goods inside the bus too much. The toy cartons were now on the floor unobtrusively near the back seat, surrounded and hidden by the musical instruments: snare drums, electric guitar and amplifier, tenor saxophone, three or four others.

Near the exit to Hilker Road, Webb stopped the bus and Stockton got out and continued down on foot. He was just barely in sight when he stopped, and they waited for the arm signal from him that would mean no traffic in sight in either direction.

It was a couple of minutes before it came, and then Webb slid the truck down the last several yards, slewed out onto the paved roadway without touching the brakes, and Stockton swung up through the open door as the bus rolled by him. Webb tapped the accelerator and they surged forward, running south.

It was a five-minute run to the South Gate. There was talk among Kengle and Stockton and Fusco on the way, but when Webb made the turn off the road and slowed to approach the gate the talk inside the bus died away and tension clogged the air like a heavy fog. It was ten after five.

Webb stopped at the gate, slid his window open, and shouted at the AP just outside. "Which way to the Officers' Club?"

The AP said something. Webb, playing it stupid, said, "Hah?" and the AP said it again. Webb said, "Hold it," turned his head, and shouted toward Parker, loud enough for the AP to hear: "He says he wants to see some authorization."

Parker took the letter out of the inside pocket of the sport jacket lying on the seat beside him. He walked up to the front of the bus, handed the letter to Webb, and Webb handed it out to the AP, saying, "This what you want?"

It had better be. The letter was written on legitimate Officers' Club letterhead stationery, stolen last Friday by Devers. It was addressed to Sheehan & Wilcox, a legitimate booking agency in New York City as gotten out of the phone book; it was signed by Major J. Alex Cartwright, which was the legitimate name of the officer in charge of the Monequois Air Force Base Officers' Club; and it requested the appearance of Ernie Seven and the Four Score for a one-night appearance at the Monequois Officers' Club on Wednesday, September 30th, at terms already agreed upon in prior correspondence. "This letter," the letter concluded, "will serve as authorization for the group's entrance onto the base on that date. We expect them no later than five p.m."

Parker watched through the window until he thought the AP had just about finished the letter, and then he leaned down past Webb and called, "Buddy, we're late now. Can we go through?"

This was the tricky part. If the AP let them through they'd be all right. If he insisted on checking with Major Cartwright at the Officers' Club the only thing for them to do was back-out of the slot, turn the truck around fast, and get the hell out of there.

The problem was the bus. They needed a vehicle in which to get the goods off the base, and if they used Devers' Pontiac it might be traced to him later. Gate guards would be encouraged to remember what vehicles left the base in the time immediately after the robbery. To simply steal a truck from the motor pool was no good unless they intended to crash out through the gate, which they wanted to avoid; they needed half an hour anyway in order to lay a false trail and get themselves to ground. So they had to have a vehicle with papers, even if the papers were false.

Which meant, before they could get the vehicle off the base, they would have to somehow get it on. Which was why all this.

Including a letter that indicated they were already ten minutes late. Over on the exit side, the gate was crowded with people who'd gotten off-duty at five o'clock. The AP should have his hands full now, the letter should convince him, the time element of their being late should encourage him to speed them through.

Maybe.

The AP frowned at the letter, squinted up at Parker and Webb in their gold tunics, looked at the banner on the side of the bus, looked at the musical instruments and the other gold-tunic'd passengers he could see through the windows, and finally said reluctantly, "I didn't hear anything about you guys."

"It's just a one-nighter for the big wheels, buddy," Webb said.

Parker said, "You want to see some identification? Driver's license? Registration?" He was ready with both, in the name of Edward Lynch, one of several sets of false papers he'd picked up here and there over the years.

Still frowning, still hesitant, the AP looked at the letter again. Then the other AP, over on the other side, called something impatient to him, and he said, more to himself than Webb and Parker, "I guess it's okay."

"Sure it's okay," Webb said. "Unless we get there too late."

"I'll get you a pass," the AP said, and walked into the shack.

Moving casually, Webb moved the shift lever into reverse.

But when the AP came out, he had a square oblong of green cardboard in his hand. "Display this in the windshield," he said, handing it up to Webb. "And you'll have to turn it back in when you leave."

"This is yours," the AP said, and handed the letter up to Webb.

"Thanks, pal. Now all we need is where's the Officers' Club."

The AP pointed the direction they were headed. "Straight down that way to G Street, then right. You can't miss it, it's the big building with the stained-glass front."

"Stained-glass front. Ain't that nice. Thanks again, pal."

Webb handed Parker the letter, put the bus in gear, and they rolled through the gate and onto the base.

Parker went back and sat down. Webb drove straight until he reached G Street, and then turned right, as the AP had said. After he made the turn, Parker and the others slipped out of their tunics and put on ties and jackets in their place. Webb kept the tunic on until he parked the bus on the cross-street between the Officers' Club on the right and the NCO Club on the left, then he too switched to tie and jacket, while Kengle and Stockton got out and removed the banner from the back of the bus. A few people walked by, in both uniform and civilian clothing but no one paid them any attention.

When Kengle and Stockton were back aboard, Webb started the bus again and drove it into the Officers' Club parking lot, putting it down at the far end, in the shade of a thick-trunked tree, one of the few trees left on the base. The other banners, tied by string to small hooks protruding from the sides of the bus, could be removed from inside by people reaching out the windows. They untied both banners, pulled them in, and rolled them carefully so as not to smear the writing on them. Then, one at a time, they left the bus and strolled across the parking lot and out to the street.

Parker went next to last, leaving Webb to lock the bus after him. It was starting to get dark with that fast-falling evening of the north country in the autumn, and about one passing car in three already had its parking lights on. Parker crossed the street and went up the walk and into the NCO Club.

Devers had said there was never any ID check at the door of the NCO Club, since the name was a misnomer. "Every base is supposed to have an airman's club," he'd said, "for the lower four grades, but I've never been on a base that does, and where there's no airman's club the NCO Club is open to all enlisted men. So when even Airman Basics can get into the NCO Club there's nobody left to keep out, so there's no check at the door."

Devers was right, there was no one there. Parker stepped inside, into a large red velvet area that could have been the lobby of a recently built theater or of a small resort hotel. Devers had told him the bar was to the left and the dining room to the right, so he went to the right along a broad hallway that continued the red velvet motif and emptied into a large rectangular dining-room, full of tables with white table cloths. At the far end was a raised platform containing a shrouded piano. Only about a quarter of the tables were occupied, mostly by men in civilian clothing. One table had four women in blue WAF uniforms, looking like chunky truck drivers.

Stockton and Kengle were at a table midway down on the left, Fusco at a closer table to the right. Parker went over and sat down with Fusco, who said, "No menu yet. That's the kind of service you get."

"We're in no hurry," Parker said. He was facing the entranceway, and a minute later saw Webb come strolling in and go over to join Stockton and Kengle. He made no sign toward Parker, which meant everything was as it should be. If there was trouble he would have managed to let Parker know it.

The waitress showed up a while later, gave them menus, took their drink orders, and left. They took their time over dinner, and then sat with drinks afterward. They drank slowly and sparingly, needing to be at their fastest and most alert later on tonight.

About six-thirty Devers came in, in civilian clothing, with three other young men about his age. They sat in a corner table and drank beer and talked urgently together. Devers never looked toward Parker nor the other table, and he drank much more slowly than his friends.

A little after eight, Parker paid the check and he and Fusco left. Devers had showed them on the map how to get from the NCO Club to the movie theater, and they strolled in that direction now.

The problem was, the rush-hour confusion around five o'clock was the best time to bring the bus in — and any arrival much later than seven would have caused suspicion anyway — but that meant they had a long time to kill before they could go after the money and leave the base again. Part of it could go to dinner, and now some more of it would be spent in a movie.

The base theater had two showings of its feature, one at eight-fifteen and one at ten-fifteen. There was a line when Parker and Fusco reached the theater at eight-ten, and they joined it. When they got their tickets and started inside they saw Webb and Stockton and Kengle just getting on the end of the line.

There was a cartoon and then the feature. It was a musical comedy, and Parker sat there and looked at the bright colors and listened to the sounds and paid it all only the slightest attention.

They cleared the theater after each showing, so they had to get back on line and pay a second time to see the movie again. This time the other three were ahead of them in the line.

Parker paid just as little attention to the movie the second time, hardly recognizing it as something he'd just seen. When it was done and the lights went on, his watch read five minutes past twelve.

It was a six-block walk back to the bus. Parker and Fusco got there first, and stood waiting for the others to come and unlock it. The Officers' Club was going strong, and where the parking lot had been almost empty before now it was full. A white MG squatted beside the bus, which was almost invisible now, its bright blue of the daytime now blending with the darkness.

The others showed up a minute or two later, and Webb unlocked the door. They climbed aboard and kept the bus in darkness. Parker changed out of his tie and jacket, putting on the long-sleeved high-neck black sweater in its place. Around him the others were putting on similar clothing, black and clean-lined, with no extraneous lapels or flaps.

Parker broke out the guns. There were two machine guns, stripped-down Stens, partly disassembled to fit into their boxes. Parker reassembled them in the dark, handed one to Kengle and one to Stockton, and then got out the pistols, all snub-nosed .32s, two Smith & Wesson, one Firearms International and one Colt. He took the Colt, gave Fusco the FI and Webb one of the S & Ws, and put the other S & W aside for Devers.

Next he got out and handed around sets of rubber gloves, the kind women use when they wash dishes. These were pale blue, which were less bright in the dark than either the yellow or the pink that were the only other choices. It was advertised that with these gloves on you could pick up a dime. You could also hold a gun and pick up four hundred thousand dollars.

There was a quick knock at the door. Webb opened it and Devers swung up and in. He too was in dark clothing, and when Parker handed him a revolver and a pair of rubber gloves he whispered, "Stage fright gone."

"Good," Parker said.

Next came the hoods, black cotton bags made from dyeing pillow cases and cutting out eyeholes. Each man stuffed his hood under his sweater, to keep it out of the way until it was needed.

Last were an Air Force fatigue cap and fatigue jacket. Webb put these on, everybody else sat out of sight on the floor, and Webb started the engine. He drove out of the parking lot and made his way slowly across the base.

It was ten minutes to one when he came to the finance office. The street was fairly well lit, and empty. There were lights on the second floor of the building, and an AP in a white helmet was marching back and forth on the sidewalk in front of the building with a carbine on his shoulder.

Devers, peeking out the window, whispered, "Is that a dumb way to guard a place? If they had him stand in front of the door they'd make a lot more sense."

Webb whispered back, "That isn't the Army way, my boy."

They were almost even with the marching AP now. When they reached him, Webb hit the brakes. The building and the AP were on the right side of the bus. Webb opened the door from the handle by the steering-wheel, leaned far over, and called, "Hey, buddy! Which way to the Motor Pool Receiving Depot?"

There was no such thing. The AP looked, saw a blue bus — like any Air Force bus, if somewhat brighter and cleaner than most — saw a driver in Air Force fatigues leaning over toward him, gripping the steering-wheel for balance, and saw nothing else to make him wonder or question. Still with the carbine on his shoulder, he took a step closer and said, "What was that?"

"The Motor Pool Receiving Depot," Webb said, slurring the last words. "I got to deliver this goddam thing sometime tonight. The stinking snowtop at the gate gave me the wrong directions."

"Snowtop?" That was a slang word for Air Policemen, because of the white helmets they wore, and most APs didn't like it. This one was no exception. Taking the carbine off his shoulder and holding it at a loose port arms, he came another step closer, almost to the curb, and said, "Maybe you heard him wrong, my friend. The motor pool isn't anywhere around here."

"I don't want the motor pool," Webb said, being angry now. "You as dumb as that other one? I want the Motor Pool Receiving Depot."

The AP was now bridling. Coming all the way to the bus door, he said, "You got any orders on you, smart guy?"

Parker was out of sight just beside the door. Now, softly, he said, "I've got one. If you're smart, you'll step up into the bus." As he spoke, he extended his hand out so the AP could see the revolver in it, aimed at his forehead.

The AP blinked. "What?"

"Come up here," Webb said, speaking more quietly himself now. "Just like there's nothing wrong."

"This isn't the war to be a hero in," Parker said.

"I don't—" The AP was squinting, trying to see up the arm past the gun. "What is this?"

"Just money," Webb told him, "We're just taking the payroll. Don't worry about it, we're not spies or saboteurs or anything."

"The payroll? You're going to steal— You'll never get away with it!"

"If you raise your voice again," Parker said, "your buddy on the other side of the building is going to hear a car backfire. Now get in here."

"But—"

"One," said Parker. "Two."

The AP didn't know what the top number was. He put his foot up on the bus step before Parker could say three.

Webb said, "Hand me the rifle."

The AP came up the steps, and anger was struggling with fear in his eyes. He was being humiliated, and he hated it, and he suspected that if he tried to do anything about the humiliation he would lose his life, and he hated the cowardice that weighed those factors and opted for cooperation. He was calling it cowardice now, in his mind, but what it was was intelligence.

Webb took the carbine from him, and Parker prodded him to move on down the aisle into the bus. His uniform was stripped off him, and Devers put it on, took the carbine from Webb, and got out of the bus.

"Thanks, buddy," Webb called, and shut the bus door, and started away.

Devers began to march up and down in front of the building. He looked bulkier than the other AP because, although he was about the other man's size, he was wearing another complete set of clothing under the borrowed uniform, complete to a snub-nosed .32 revolver in the hip pocket of the trousers. But to anyone passing by, or to either of the APs inside the building upstairs who might decide to look out a window, he would pass.

Webb drove straight for a block and a half, turned right for one block, turned right again, and parked. Meanwhile the AP had been put down in the aisle in his underwear and tied and gagged.

Stockton, wearing his hood and carrying his Sten gun, got out of the bus and moved away in the darkness like a long thin shadow. Three strides from the bus he was out of sight, these side streets being lit only by overflow from the lights at the intersections with the main avenues.

There was a second guard on duty behind the building, and this was who Stockton had gone after.

He brought him back three minutes later, a young scared boy, his face almost as white as his helmet. Stockton held the Sten gun in his right hand, butt braced against his hip bone, with the boy's carbine hanging loose in his left hand.

They tied and gagged number two, left him in the bus with the first one, and they all moved off except Webb, who was to stay with the bus, move it if it seemed necessary and keep an eye on the two APs.

Parker led the way through the darkness. The sky was clear and full of stars, but they were only three days from the new moon, so that only a thin curved sliver, like a fingernail clipping in light, showed to mark where the moon would be a few nights from now.

They came at the finance office building from the rear, moved around it on the side between it and the other building on that block, and at the front corner waited, the others strung behind Parker, who watched Devers marching back and forth out there with the same stoop-shouldered fatalistic tread as the boy he was replacing.

Parker stepped around the corner, stood against the front of the building. He showed there as a dark man-shaped shadow against the stucco wall. His hood was on, the only pale thing about him were the rubber gloves on his hands. He moved these back and forth in front of himself, fingers splayed, until Devers saw the motion. Then he stopped marching, yawned, stretched, and walked over to the building entrance in the middle of the long front wall. He stood there and lit a cigarette, the signal that it was all right to come on.

Parker had Devers' bootleg keys in his hand when he reached the door. He unlocked it and stepped through, stood just inside holding the door, and felt the other three slide in behind him. Devers, who had said nothing and who had looked ashen-faced beneath the helmet, field-stripped his cigarette and went back out to march up and down on the sidewalk some more.

Devers had given them complete maps of the building. Parker and the others moved without hesitation through the darkness to the stairs and up, their shoes silent on the metal stairs.

The door to the left at the head of the stairs had glass in the upper half. Through it, Parker could see two overhead globes lit, both down at the far end of the finance office; the one inside Major Creighton's office and the first one on the right on this side of the Major's office. The two APs on guard here were sitting at a desk under this second light, playing cards. They were about twenty-five feet from the door where Parker was standing, and the area between was lined with two rows of desks up to a chest-high counter which stretched across the room about six feet in from the door. To the left of the door was a bench for people who had to wait.

Parker used another key, opened the door with a faint click timed to happen when one of the APs was shuffling the cards, and, as down there under the light a new gin rummy hand was dealt out, Parker and the other three slid through the slightly open door and moved at a half-crouch to the counter. They straightened slowly and stood spread out there, Kengle and Stockton at the ends with the Sten guns resting on the countertop, Parker and Fusco in the middle with their revolvers in their hands. Ahead of them, the APs continued to be absorbed in their game.

A cord was hanging down over Parker's head. He reached

up with his free hand and pulled it, and the globe up there came on, flooding their end of the room with light.

The APs looked over, startled.

"Freeze," Parker said.

One of them would have, but the other was a cowboy. He made a lunge for where his carbine was leaning against another desk, and Kengle's Sten gun rattled briefly. The AP half-turned in midair, slid over the desk, and crumpled like used cardboard on the other side.

The shots shook the other one, who had frozen the way Parker told him to. He abruptly dropped out of sight behind the desk.

Parker said, "Don't be stupid, son. You don't want to die."

Nothing happened.

Parker nodded at Stockton, who was nearest the flap in the counter. He pushed it up, left it up, and went on through. Moving fast and silent, he went down along the rear wall, where he wouldn't be seen by anybody passing in the street, and when he got to where the second AP had disappeared he waved to the others that it was all right.

When they walked down to him, they saw that AP number two hadn't ducked, he'd fainted. AP number one wasn't dead, but his breathing was shallow and his color bad. He had one hit in the left side, just above the waist, and one that had gone in his left shoulder and out his back above the shoulder blade. Fusco used some of the boy's clothing to make simple bandages to stop the bleeding; they weren't in a hurry for a murder rap. The law might think it looks as hard for every kind of felon, but it doesn't. Just as the cop killer is tracked with more savagery and singlemindedness than is the ordinary killer, the ordinary killer in his turn is hunted more fiercely than is the robber.

Stockton used the rope and handkerchief he'd brought to tie AP number two, and even though AP number one looked to be out for it for the rest of the night, Fusco did the same for him. Meantime Parker helped Kengle out of the small knapsack he'd put on just before leaving the bus.

The knapsack contained tools: drill, various bits, screwdrivers, two hammers, a chisel, some other things. With it all, while Stockton kept an eye on Devers and the street and Fusco watched the two APs up here, Parker and Kengle went to work on the vault.

"Vault" was a little too grand a name for it, but on the other hand "safe" was too small a word. It was like a reinforced metal closet in one corner of the room, with a heavy rectangular vault door on it. There was no point trying to go through the wall, so Parker and Kengle concentrated on the door itself, on the combination lock and the hinges.

The hinges proved to be impossible to get at, no matter how they drilled. The weak spot was in the lock. With a combination of drilling and sawing they managed to remove it completely, leaving a hole they could reach into and get at the lock components on the inside. The whole job of opening the door took forty-five minutes.

When the door was open, they saw several metal shelves. The floor was higher than the office floor, because it was reinforced, and on it were two large metal cases, side by side, filling up the whole space. These were what the payroll had arrived in by air this morning. Parker and Kengle pulled them out and opened them.

Several of the shelves were lined with metal boxes, dark green, like long squared-off tool kits, and in each of these was the payroll for a different organization on the base. There was too much bulk and weight to carry all these separate boxes, so Kengle and Parker now went to work forcing each of them open and dumping the money into the larger crates. In each box, beside two or three stacks of bills with red rubber bands around them, there were always a few rolls of coins and a list from a computer giving each man's name and how much money he was to receive. Only the bills went into the crates, the coins and lists being discarded with the boxes.

It took another half hour to unload all the boxes, and when they were unloaded the two crates were both about three-quarters full. It was now two-fifteen; they'd been at work an hour and a quarter. In that time, Devers had not had cause at all to high-sign Stockton. This part of the base was strictly offices, and deserted at night. And tonight, just before payday besides being a week night, there weren't very many men with the money or inclination to be out for any reason. They had the area to themselves.

The crates had been pretty heavy to start with, being made of steel, and now that they were full of money they were a full two-man job each. Parker and Fusco took one, Kengle and Stockton took the other, and they moved out of the office and down through the blackness to the first floor.

Parker lit a match in the doorway, and when Devers saw it he stopped and shifted his carbine to port arms. He stood there, his back to the building as he watched in both directions, and Parker and the others carried the two crates out, hurried along the front of the building with them and around the corner into the deeper darkness between the buildings. Here they put them down to rest for a minute, and out front Devers went back to his marching.

From the side of the building to the bus was fast and easy, in solid darkness. Webb opened the door for them and they piled the cases aboard, then carried the two APs out and put them under some bushes at the side of a building across the street, where it was unlikely they'd be found before morning.

When they got back to the bus Webb had put the rear banner on again. They quickly put the side banners on and climbed aboard. Webb had discarded his fatigue jacket and cap and switched to his gold tunic. Now, as the bus started forward, the others got out of their hoods and black sweaters and put their own tunics back on.

Webb turned the corner, stopped for a second, and Devers swung on, grinning from ear to ear, "Beautiful," he said.

"Get changed," Fusco told him. It wasn't over yet.

Devers quit grinning. He shucked out of the borrowed uniform, put his tunic on, and rolled the uniform and carbine and helmet and Webb's fatigue cap and jacket into a ball. Webb stopped on one dark street and Devers went out to stow these things in a litter basket. Then they drove on.

By the time they reached the South Gate the money crates

were stowed way in back, hidden by the musical instruments. The machine guns were back there, too, but the four revolvers were still in pockets, close to hand, when Webb pulled to a stop beside the AP shack.

The guard who came out was young and heavy-lidded. Webb handed the pass to him and the guard looked at it with sleepy suspicion. "You guys are leaving awful late," he said.

"We were a smash, pal," Webb told him. "They wouldn't let us go."

"Sure." He waved them through, saying, "Okay, go ahead."

"Right, pal."

Out on Hilker Road they turned left and accelerated. There was no traffic anywhere. The speedometer touched ninety, and in under three minutes Webb slowed for the dirt road. This time he went up as fast as the road and bus would take it, not caring how much he jounced the contents or the passengers. Parker and the others clung to seat backs and got bounced around.

At the top, Webb stopped in front of the garages. Stockton ducked out to open one of the doors and Parker and Fusco and Devers and Kengle carried the two crates out and put them in the garage. While they were doing that, Webb turned the bus around and Stockton opened the other garage doors.

Devers said, "See you next week." The plan was that he was to meet Fusco in New York in ten days to get his piece of the pie.

"See you, Stan," Fusco said.

Devers got into his Pontiac while Parker slid behind the wheel of Webb's station wagon. Webb had already started back down the slope.

Parker went second down the dirt road in the Buick, with Devers behind him. At the bottom, Devers blinked his lights in farewell and headed south while Parker turned north after the disappearing taillights of the bus.

They took it up to within two miles of the border, where Webb ran it deep off the road into a stand of trees where it couldn't be seen from the road. But the tracks would be seen. The law would find the bus early tomorrow, probably within an hour of the alert going out. They would believe the bandits had gone over the border into Canada.

Parker turned the wagon round and slid over to the passenger side. Webb opened the door, got in behind the wheel, and headed them south again. "Worked out nice," he said.

"It did," Parker said.

Neither of them was much of a talker, so they were quiet after that. Parker liked that about Webb, his close-mouthedness. They'd worked together a couple of times several years ago, and all Parker knew about Webb was that he was a good hard driver, that he had a passion for playing with cars, and that he was solid in a pinch. It was all he needed to know.

After they made the turn now they stopped and, in the red glow of the taillights, smeared away the tracks their tires had made. They didn't want anybody coming up here for any reason in the next few days. For the same reason, they stopped again partway up, spent a while brushing away more tracks, and dragged a heavy branch back across the road where it had been before Parker and Fusco had removed it the other day. Then they drove the rest of the way up.

The darkness at the top was complete, broken only by their headlights. All the garage doors were shut.

Webb and Parker got out and opened a set of garage doors and there wasn't anybody there. Kengle and Stockton and Fusco, all gone. And the money gone too.

Part Four

1

PARKER FOUND them both in the bedroom. Up until one second ago they'd been having sex, and when Parker hit the light switch Devers came up off the bed, looking as foolish as a naked man can look. Ellen blinked in terror at the light.

Parker looked at Ellen and said, "She still here."

Devers said, "Parker?" He was still too shocked to be able to think. "What's going on?"

Parker ignored him. He went over to the foot of the bed and said to Ellen, "Didn't you think I'd tip?"

"What— what—"

"Parker," Devers said. "For Christ's sake—"

"It's gone," Parker told him. "Webb and I ditched the bus, went back to the lodge, and the cash was gone."

Webb, still in the doorway, said quietly, "Three dead, pal."

Devers just blinked. "Dead?"

"Fusco," Parker said. "And Stockton. And Kengle."

Webb said, "We found them over by the workshed. They'd been lined up and shot down."

Devers and Ellen were both beginning to unscramble their brains now. Ellen reached for a blanket to cover herself, and Devers said, "We were hijacked? It's gone?"

"Somebody hit us for the bundle," Parker said. "They had to be waiting up there for us."

"In the workshed," Webb said.

"Wherever it was," Parker said, not caring. "They waited for us to show up, they waited for you to go and me and Webb to go. They waited till the one time when there'd be only three men on the stash."

Webb said, "You know what that means, buddy?"

"They had to know," Devers said. His face was bloodless, there was no strength in his voice.

"They had to know the whole caper," Webb said.

"In advance," Parker said.

"Right," Webb said. "They had to know not only we were scoring tonight, they had to know where the hideout was and when we were due to get there and how we were going to split up then, with Parker and me off to get rid of the bus and you coming back here."

Devers said, "It had to be somebody on the inside." He sat down on the edge of the bed, dropping there as though his legs wouldn't hold him any more. "You think it's me," he said. He looked hopeless, as though it didn't seem to him there was any way to keep them from thinking it was him and acting on that assumption.

Parker said, "I don't think you're that stupid, Devers. You don't want to be hunted, not by the cops and not by us. If you work a cross on us, you can't hang around, you've got to clear out. If you clear out, you're a deserter from the Air Force. If you desert the day after the heist, they know you were in on it. That isn't what you want."

Webb said, "I'll tell you the truth, Devers, I'm not as sold as Parker. I think you're young and cocky, I think you just might try it, figure you could stick around and look innocent and bewildered when we show up."

"Sixty-five thousand is enough," Devers said to him. "That's the only point, sixty-five thousand is plenty. If I've got sixty-five thousand dollars I'm not hungry enough to go up against you five guys."

"That's a point in your favor," Webb said. "And I don't think you could have taken those three out at the lodge by yourself. But why bump them unless it was somebody they knew and could remember? You see the kind of question I ask myself. Maybe you had a couple buddies from the air base stashed up there, helping you out."

"So I split with them? What difference does it make who split with if all I get is a piece anyway?"

"Webb moved the hand that didn't have a gun in it. "You're probably clean," he said. "All I'm saying, I'm not as one hundred per cent sold as Parker."

"Sure," Devers said. He was getting his wits about him more and more now. "If it isn't me," he said, "you're stuck. There's nobody left."

Parker gestured his revolver at Ellen. "Was she here when you came back?"

Ellen had been staring at Parker wide-eyed all the time, clutching the blanket around herself. She was huddled up against the headboard of the bed, her mouth was slack with terror, and there was no way to tell whether she'd heard or understood a word that had been said, except that she flinched now when Parker moved the gun and referred to her.

Devers looked at Parker in astonishment, then at Ellen, then back at Parker. "Sure she was. Ellen? You don't think she—"

"She's the one," Parker said.

"She was here. And she wouldn't set up something like that, for God's sake. Kill Marty? Why?"

Ellen said something, muffled and jumbled. They all looked at her and she said it again: "Marty isn't dead."

Parker said to Devers, "She set it up. I don't know why, maybe not for the money, maybe just to keep you from getting into another of these things, maybe she's not taking a piece at all. But she turned somebody loose on us, gave them the whole thing. She almost told me about it this afternoon, she was nervous, acting weird, afraid to go through with it."

Devers was steadily shaking his head, and now he said, "Parker, Ellen wouldn't do a thing like that. She isn't that kind of woman, she'd never fink on anybody like that."

Webb said, "That's why I'm not a hundred per cent solid on you, pal. Because I don't think she's right to play finger either."

Parker said to her. "Where are they? Tell us where they are, I won't touch you. I'll leave Devers to figure out what to do with you. That won't be much trouble, he loves you. Where are they?"

"Marty isn't dead,"she said.

Parker said, "Devers, slap her face. I want her awake."

But then Ellen shrieked, "Why would he *do* a thing like that?" Face contorted with rage, she leaped off the bed and tried to run out of the room. Parker grabbed her and she twisted and squirmed, trying to get away, shouting, "I've got to talk to him, I've got to find out! I've got to know why he did it, why he'd *do* something like that!"

Parker slapped her with his free hand, open palm across the face, and she sagged against him, her body abruptly boneless. Holding her up, Parker said, "Who? Who did it?"

"I was supposed to be able to trust him," she said, her eyes closed, her body slack with defeat.

Parker shook her. "Who?"

Devers said, "For Christ's sake, Parker, don't you get it. She's talking about her analyst!"

At the sound of the word Ellen tensed again, but she kept her eyes closed and continued to sag against Parker's chest. Over her shoulder Parker said to Devers, "Why?"

"She told him the whole dodge," Devers said. "Don't you see? Not to set up anything against us, but because it was shaking her up. She figured she could trust him, it was like going to confession, she spilled the whole thing to the son of a bitch."

"You know where he lives?"

"I know where his office is."

"Where's a phone book?"

"Unlisted," Ellen said. It was a near-whisper, almost a sigh.

Parker held her out where he could look at her lolling face and closed eyes. He said, "What's the home address?"

"I don't know, he won't tell, he doesn't want patients bothering him late at night."

Parker shoved Ellen over to Webb, saying, "Tie her." To Devers he said, "Get dressed."

"What are we going to do?"

"We've got till first light, if we're lucky, to get it back and get ourselves out of sight."

Devers reached for his clothing.

2

THE PLATE beside the door read: *Monequois Professional Building*. On the other side was a white painted board with a list of the tenants in black lettering: doctors, lawyers and a firm of accountants. Dr Fred Godden's name was fourth from the top.

The building was of fairly recent construction, red brick with white trim, built in a neighbourhood gradually changing over from expensive homes to expensive offices. Air conditioners stuck their squared-off crenelated black rumps out of most of the windows, and there were bushes planted across the front of the building, plus a small well-kept lawn extending out to the street. And more than enough illumination; in addition to the streetlight just across the way, a pair of carriage lamps bracketing the front entrance were kept burning all night.

There was a blacktop driveway beside the building. Webb had switched his headlights off three blocks ago, and when he reached the building now he kept them off as he turned the Buick into the driveway and aimed for the blackness beside the building. Brick wall went by on their left, a high hedge on their right, both unseen. When the tires left blacktop and crunched on gravel Webb hit the brakes and cut the ignition.

They were all three in the front seat, Devers in the middle. Parker opened the door and got out and Devers slid out after him. Webb left the car on the other side. No interior light went on when the car doors were open. Leaving them open, they moved away through almost perfect darkness to the brick rear wall of the building and felt their way to the rear door.

If they'd had to go through without leaving any marks it might have taken half an hour or more, but now they didn't care about marks, only about time. They went through the door in three minutes and moved quickly up the stairs to the second floor.

The office doors had frosted glass in their upper panels, names on the glass in gold letters. Behind the one that read DR FRED GODDEN, small yellowish red light glowed.

Standing against the wall out of direct line of the doorway, Parker tried the knob. When he pushed, the door gave. It was unlocked.

All three had revolvers in their hands. Devers had left his at the lodge to be disposed of, but Parker had brought it back to him.

Parker pushed the door slowly. There was no pressure wanting to close it, but it didn't swing loosely, probably because it needed oiling or adjusting. It opened willingly as far as Parker would push it, but no more.

When it was halfway open, Parker eased his head over until he could look one-eyed through the opening. He saw a pie wedge of outer office, a corner of Naugahyde sofa, a part of a desk, a partially open door across the way. The light was coming from that inner room.

There was no sound. Parker pushed the door open the rest of the way, hesitated, stepped inside. Nobody here, not in this outer room.

Devers and Webb followed him in. They came cautiously at the next door and again Parker leaned into it from the side, the revolver ready in his hand, his other hand flat against the wall behind him to lever him back out of the way if it was needed.

Another pie slice. A desk again, this one larger. Patterned carpet. Glassfronted bookcases. The light came from a table lamp with an orange shade, sitting on one corner of the desk.

Again no sound, nothing moving. Parker entered as carefully as before, and still nothing happened.

Now he could see the rest of the room. A sofa along the left wall, an armchair at its far end. A couple more lamps, a library table, a filing cabinet, a coffee table in front of the sofa.

A sound. From behind the desk.

Parker dropped. He lay on the rug, listening, and when he turned his head and looked across the carpet into the darkness under the desk and beyond the desk, near where the wheeled legs of the office chair came down, he saw a pair of eyes, blinking whitely.

Sideways. Someone lying on his back, head turned this way, eyes slowly opening and closing.

Parker got to his feet. Behind him to the left was a wall switch. He hit it, and indirect lighting filled the room from troughs along the top of the walls. He went around behind the desk as Webb and Devers came in.

The man on the floor was tall, muscular with an overlay of flab. He was wearing scuffed brown oxfords, baggy brown trousers, a bulky dark-green sweater frayed here and there. The sweater was caked and smeared dark brown in two places over his chest and stomach. A dark slender ribbon glinted along his cheek from his mouth, disappeared into his hair beneath his ear. He must have been lying with his head tilted a little the other way for a while. Maybe he'd heard Parker and the others coming in, had managed to turn his head. He wasn't moving now.

Devers had come around the desk from the other side, stood with his shoes near the guy's head. He said. "Dead?"

"Not yet. You know him?"

"I don't think so. I can't see his face."

Parker went on one knee beside the wounded man, put his hand on the guy's chin, turned his head so Devers could see it. Blood had started to trickle out the other side of the mouth now. His eyes were open again. They blinked, very slowly, shut and then open. They did it again. When they were open the eyes didn't focus on anything, just looked straight ahead at the ceiling. They kept blinking at the same slow steady rhythm.

Devers looked sick. He shook his head. "No," he said. "I don't know who he is."

"You never saw him at all?"

"Never. I'd remember."

Parker let the chin go, and the head stayed where he'd left it. Some blood was on the first finger of Parker's left hand. He cleaned it on the guy's sweater, then pushed the body partway over to get at the hip pocket, where the wallet should be.

It was there. Parker opened it, found a driver's license, read the name aloud. "Ralph Hochberg. Mean anything?"

"Nothing," Devers said.

Hochberg's head was facing front again, his eyes staring at the ceiling, blinking slowly without let-up. He began to gurgle in his throat,a small damp choking sound.

Devers said, "He's strangling on his blood."

Parker pushed Hochberg's face to the side, so the blood could flow out, and got to his feet. "They were here," he said, more to himself than Devers. "Godden and this one. Just the two of them? They've started to doublecross each other."

"Godden wouldn't try it with just one other man," Devers said. "Not going up against three pros, even with surprise on his side. He'd want to make it three against three at least. More, if he could find the people. You suppose this guy's a patient of his?"

Webb came over, an envelope in his hand. He'd been searching the room and going through the filing-cabinet while Parker and Devers concentrated on the wounded man. Webb said, "Nobody else. The cases are over there, past the sofa. Empty."

"This is where they divvied," Parker said.

"I found this," Webb said, handing out the envelope.

Parker took it. It was addressed to Dr Fred Godden, 16 Rosemont Road, West Monequois, New York. That wasn't the office address.

Parker handed the envelope to Devers, saying, "You know this town. Would that be a residence?"

"Sure," Devers said. "West Monequois, that's high class."

Webb said, "Let's go there."

3

ROSEMONT ROAD curved gracefully back and forth among brick ranches and frame split levels, each on its own grassy lot, with its wide driveway, attached garage, TV antenna and sloped roof. It was almost three-thirty in the morning now, and every house they passed was completely dark, except that every now and then a night light showed faintly through a window.

Number sixteen was on the right, a split level with the garage in the lower part of the two-storey section. It was as dark as the rest of the neighborhood, a white frame house built up on a rise of land above the road, with a steep rock garden at the front of the lawn, a broad driveway that angled upward sharply, and a look of innocence and sleep.

Webb drove on until the curve of the road hid them from the Godden house, and then he parked. All three got out and walked back along the sidwalk, cutting across the lawn of the house next door in order to come at the Godden house from the back, on the garage side.

There was a door at the back of the house, leading into the garage. They approached it slowly, the darkness as deep as velvet all around them, the house a vaguely seen pale shape looming up in front of them. They were silent, moving on grass. They reached the rear wall and slid along it to the door.

Parker tried the knob. It clicked faintly, but the door was locked.

A voice said, "Roger?"

Parker flattened against the house.

The voice was above him, somebody in a second-storey

window. It said, "I don't want to hurt you, Roger." It was a male voice, but womanish and trembling with fear.

Parker waited.

The voice said, "I have a gun. You'd better get away from here."

Moving slowly, Parker turned his head. He could see that Webb was no longer there behind him, which was good. Devers, a few feet away, was pressed close to the wall just as Parker was.

The voice said, "You've got all the money, what more do you want?"

Whispers don't have much individuality. Making his shrill, Parker whispered, "Ralph is still alive!"

"What do you want *me* to do about it?" The voice was getting shrill itself, the tension in it twanged like a plucked zither string.

"Help him," Parker whispered.

"*Help* him! Why *shoot* him? What's the matter with you?"

"I need your help," Parker whispered. "Let me in."

"So you can kill me, too?"

"Why would I kill you?"

"Why did you shoot Ralph? Roger, I'm sorry, I can't trust you. Maybe tomorrow. What are we going to do about Ralph? I thought he was dead. I though I'd have to go back later and take him out and leave his body somewhere. But if he's alive, I—" With sudden suspicion, the voice said, "Is he alive? How do you know?"

"I went back."

"How did you know where to find me? Roger? *Is that Roger down there?*"

"Yes." If Devers was right, that Godden's partners were probably patients of his, a little hysteria might be in order now. Parker suddenly rattled the doorknob loudly, whispering, "Let me in! I threw the gun away, I don't want to kill anybody any more! Let me in! I need your help!"

"That isn't Roger!"

Where the hell was Webb? "Help me!" Parker whispered, flapping his arms against the door, moving around like someone too agitated to stand still. Or like someone trying to be a bad target.

There was a sudden light from above, and Parker was in the middle of it. A flashlight. Parker dove for the darkness and above him a rifle sounded, loud and flat.

Parker landed on his shoulder, rolled, got to his feet in darkness, with the flashlight aimed out past where he was. He ran in close again, against the wall, and suddenly the flashlight dropped from the window and landed on the grass. It lay there, still lit, shining with great precision and clarity on a cone of green grass.

Parker saw the outline of Devers on the other side of the light, moving toward it. He whispered, "Keep away!" and Devers faded back again.

Nothing happened for almost a minute, and then Webb's voice came from up above, softly, saying, "Clear."

"There's got to be other people in the house," Parker said, speaking just as softly. "Cover them."

"Right. I came in the garage window on the side of the house. People never lock that one."

Parker and Devers went around to the side where there was a smallish window, now standing open. They climbed through, landing in a mass of garden hose, edged around some kind of long broad car, and went through a doorway and up a half-flight of stairs to a kitchen.

There was light now, filtering from another part of the house. Moving toward it, they left the kitchen through an arched doorway, turned right down a short hall, and went up another half-flight of stairs. There was another short hall up here, with light spilling from a doorway on the right.

It was a bedroom, done in colonial, with a canopy bed. Webb was standing by the foot of the bed, revolver in his hand. Sitting on the floor was a balding man of about forty-five, dressed in pajamas. There was a gash on the side of his head, bleeding slightly. He'd touched it at one point, and now there was blood on his fingertips. He looked frightened, and calculating.

When Parker and Devers came into the room, Webb said,

"Nobody else here. Empty kid's room across the way."

Parker said to the man on the floor, "Where's your family?"

"I'm remarried. My children live with my ex-wife."

"Where's your new wife?"

"Visiting her brother. I didn't want her around during—" He gestured vaguely.

Webb nodded and said, "Didn't want to have to tell her where he was going at two o'clock in the morning."

Parker said, "You're Godden?"

The man nodded wearily. "Of course."

"Ellen Fusco told you the caper."

"Yes. And I tried to steal the money away from you." He looked up, squinting. "I almost made it, too," he said. "Except Roger went crazy."

"Roger who?"

"Roger St Cloud. A local boy."

"Like Ralph?"

"Is he really still alive?"

"He was when we were there. Maybe he isn't now. Were they both patients of yours?"

"Yes. I didn't have anything to do with killing your friends."

Parker said, "It was all Roger."

"He swore one of them reached for a gun. The tall thin one. He was guarding them while Ralph and I put the money cases in the car." Godden shook his head, frowning. "I don't know how he could have been reaching for a gun," he said. "We'd already searched them all, we had their guns."

Parker said, "What happened at the office?"

"We'd been arguing. I said he didn't have to shoot all three of them, even if one did reach for a gun. We got to the office, and split up the money. We had suitcases there, we'd already each brought a suitcase and left it in the office. Everything was fine, and then Roger started up again, about how he'd been given the dangerous job, how I'd known those were dangerous men and they'd try something and he'd have to kill them. Blaming me, you see. And then deciding what

I meant to do was turn him over to the police for murder,and then Ralph and I would split his share between us. It was all very obvious, justifying what he meant to do by blaming us in advance."

Devers said, "Cut out the shoptalk, Doc. What happened?"

"Yes," Godden said, and nodded wearily. "Ralph said something. I don't know, something innocuous, Ralph was never anything but innocuous. Something about how Roger didn't really mean all that. And Roger didn't say a word. He just went over to the sofa and picked up the rifle and shot Ralph. Ralph came staggering back by the desk, still on his feet, and Roger shot him again. That's how I got away. Without the money."

Godden seemed done. Parker prodded him, saying, "What next!"

"I got the car and drove home. I didn't think Roger would be able to find out where I lived, at least not tonight. I didn't know if anyone had heard the shots, so I came home and put the car away and got ready for bed. In case the police showed up, you know, to say there was somebody dead in my office. So I wouldn't know anything about it. But I couldn't sleep, I kept prowling around in the dark in here, and then I heard you people at the back door. I thought it was Roger."

Parker said, "You soured a very sweet operation tonight, Doctor."

Godden peered up at him again. "You're Parker, aren't you?" he said. "Ellen described you very well."

"Time for you to describe your boy Roger," Parker said. "I want to know what he looks like, where he lives, and what he's going to do next."

"How should I know what he's going to do next?"

"You're his analyst. Analyze him."

Godden managed a nervous smile. "It's not that simple," he said.

Parker turned to Webb. "You two look the place over. In case this bird got the boodle after all."

"I really didn't."

As Webb and Devers left the room, Parker sat down on the edge of the bed. "Roger St Cloud," he said. "Tell me about him."

Godden licked his lips, touched again the still-oozing wound in his forehead. He sighed. "Roger's twenty-two, about six feet tall, very thin. Acne on his face, very bad. His father's a banker in town."

"Address?"

"Uhhhh, 123 Haines Avenue."

"Will he go there?"

"I don't know. He's very erratic, very unreliable. You see how badly I misjudged him tonight. I thought I could control him, but I couldn't. He'd never had power before, you see. And there he was, standing there with the rifle in his hand and three men in front of him, completely in his power. He had to use it, he had to try it out."

Parker said, "I want to know if he'll go home. What was he going to do with his share, you ever talk about that with him?"

"He had different plans at different times. He was going to go to New York, or Hollywood, or Europe, he didn't know where."

"But he was going to leave town."

"It wasn't real to him," Godden said. "He didn't know what he was going to do."

"Does he have a car?"

"A motorcycle."

"Did he have it at the office tonight?"

"No. I picked him up in my car, near his house."

Parker sat back and tried to figure it. There were three suitcases full of cash. This Roger wasn't going to load all that on a motorcycle. The way the timing worked, he couldn't have gotten out of the office more than about fifteen minutes before Parker and the others arrived. And he was on foot then.

With three suitcases?

Parker said, "Does his father have a car?" When Godden

didn't answer right away, Parker looked at him and saw an odd expression on his face, startled, absorbed, as though he was seeing something in the middle distance that he didn't at all like.

Parker said, "What is it?"

His voice hushed, Godden said, "I think I know what Roger's going to do."

4

"THE DOC called it," Devers said.

They were on Haines Avenue, and they'd pulled to the curb a block from the house where Godden had said Roger St Cloud lived. Down there, a block away, at just about the right location to be house number 123, there was all the light in the world, contrasting with the darkness here where Parker and Devers and Webb sat in the front seat of the station wagon and looked out the windshield at all the activity.

There was plenty of activity. At the intersection between here and the St Cloud house there was a patrolman in uniform, standing in the middle of the street, prepared to divert all traffic from continuing on down Haines Avenue. Beyond him three police cars — one black municipal police car and two black and white State Trooper cars — were stopped at angles across the street, their doors hanging open. Beyond that there was a large searchlight mounted on a truck bed, the light on and beamed directly at the house that had to be 123. Uniformed policemen moved in vague spurts on the opposite side of the street, and every once in a while there was the isolated sound of a shot.

It was nearly four o'clock in the morning now, but a crowd had already formed on the sidewalks on this side of the intersection, jostling each other to get a better look. From a few cars parked along the curb, and the number of people in robes, they were probably still mostly neighborhood residents, most likely including people evacuated from the houses right around the St Cloud place. If there were local all-night radio a lot more people would be crowding around the perimeter of the action by now, turning Roger St Cloud's death throes into live television.

What Dr Godden had said was, "He'll kill his father," And when Parker asked him why, Godden said, "That's the only reason he needs power, to free himself from his father. He's used clothing, the motorcycle, sarcasm, all limited forms of power, all aimed at his father. Now he's got real power. He's tested it, and proved it works. He has three hundred and eighty thousand dollars, which is another kind of power, his father's kind of power, and he's going to want to go away and try using that power, too, but first he's going to want to use the power on his father.

Parker said, "The rifle."

"Yes. The first thing he'll do is go home and shoot his father. May I use the phone?"

"No."

"But there may still be a chance to warn him."

"You mean tip him."

"The father I'm talking about."

"The son I'm talking about," Parker told him, and then they tied Dr Godden and left his house and drove here, and a block away a searchlight borrowed from the air base was flooding white light onto the St Cloud house, policemen crouched behind automobile fenders were shooting at an upstairs window, and a hundred people were standing on the sidelines and watching.

Webb said, "That's it."

"Wait a while," Parker said.

Devers said, "Let's get out, move a little closer."

"We can see from here," Parker told him.

Webb added, "Without anybody seeing us."

Someone was using a loudhailer. They could hear it plainly, but just as noise, not broken into words. But they didn't have to hear the words to know what Roger St Cloud was being told.

Several windows had been lit on this block when they'd arrived, and now that the loudhailer had started up more windows were springing into yellow light. The law couldn't have gotten here more than five minutes before Parker and the other two. That was better than the other way around.

They watched for three or four minutes. The loudhailer spoke, was silent a while, spoke again, was silent again. Policemen dodged from car fender to car fender, with no apparent destination. It seemed as though everybody was just milling around.

"They'll think of tear gas in a little while," Webb said.

Parker nodded. "It'll be on its way already,"

In the meantime there was sporadic gunfire, with long seconds of silence. The law was using different kinds of gun, revolvers and rifles and at least one riot gun that twice made its monkey jabber, hemstitching a line of bullets across the front of the house.

St Cloud was firing back, too. A policeman went running, crouching, zigzagging across a bit of open space, and then crumpled and somersaulted and lay spread out on the ground. There was a hail of answering fire, and under its cover two cops ran out, grabbed the fallen one by the arms and dragged him back out of the line of fire.

After that there was another period of silence, with here and there a shot as though just to keep up appearances.

Webb said, "Why don't he hit the light?"

"He doesn't want to get away," Devers said. "He wants to kill people."

Webb frowned. "Why?"

The loudhailer spoke again. When it was still they could hear another sound, high-pitched, twanging, shrill. Devers whispered, "That's him. Listen to him."

"It don't sound human," said Webb. He looked past Devers at Parker. "Let's get out of here. He's got our cash, he's surrounded by cops, it's all up."

Parker said, "Look."

They looked. Snow was fluttering out of an upstairs window in the house, paper snow, cascading out, glide-glide-gliding to the ground like leaves, green leaves, pouring and billowing out of the window.

Webb said, "Our money."

"It's what Godden said," Devers said, as though to himself. "He's using power."

"What the hell is he trying for?" Webb wanted to know. He was getting mad.

"He's buying them off," Devers told him. "He's crazy as a loon in there, he's using up all his power at once, killing people, buying them off."

A suitcase had come flying out of the window, spilling the rest of its cash, bills flapping down, tossed by breezes. The people held back at the intersection by the police line didn't know yet what it was, they just kept watching.

More money came out of the window, and then a second suitcase, open like the first, shooting out of the window as though catapulted, turning over and over in the air, spewing money out in gobs and flurries.

Then nothing happened. Nothing at all. The second suitcase hit the ground not far from the first, the money fluttered slowly downward through the air, that was all.

The shrill voice started again, its words as indistinguishable as the loudhailer's, but the voice that drowned it out was as clear as glass. It was a voice from the spectators, and what it shouted was: "That's *money!*"

Everthing seemed to stop. The shrill voice kept on, saying whatever it had to say, but nobody was listening any more. Everybody was tensed, everybody knew what was going to happen, everybody was waiting for whatever the signal was going to be.

The policemen across from the house were all looking down this way now, toward the crowd, and in the harsh light their faces looked pale and tense and worried.

Webb said, "They're going to—"

The crowd broke.

One second they'd all been back, standing there, straining forward but staying outside the perimeter the police had set up for them. The next second they were all in motion, rushing forward across the intersection and into the bath of light, down on their hands and knees, clutching handfuls of money, swarming on the lawn, the sidewalk, the driveway.

"That's our money," Webb said. He glared through the windshield at the mass of people.

Devers pointed higher. "Look at him!"

He was a black comma, leaning out a second-storey window, and the vertical line was a rifle. He was firing into the crowd under him, plinking away, quickly but methodically.

There were screams from down below now, and some people ran back out of the light, but most of them stayed there, scrabbling for the bills, ignoring everything else.

Parker looked across the street, saw a uniformed cop there with a rifle to his shoulder. He was damn finicky, under the circumstances, taking his time, being extra sure of his aim. With all the noise, Parker couldn't hear the sound of the shot, but he saw the rifle kick in the cop's hands. He looked back and saw St Cloud drop into the people. "All right," he said. "Let's get out of here."

"Right." Webb put the Buick into gear, made a tight U-turn, and they headed away from there.

Devers, disappointment thick in his voice, said, "What now?"

"Godden's office," Parker said.

Webb leaned forward to glance at him past Devers, then looked straight again, saying, "Why?"

"Because two suitcases went out the window," Parker said. "There were three. He was on foot and two was all he could manage. The third one is hidden around there somewhere handy."

"Son of a bitch," said Webb, and leaned on the accelerator.

5

"It's here!" Devers shouted, and the other two came running.

They hadn't worried about noise or light this trip; time was the important element now. With the Buick sitting with its high beams on in the middle of the gravel parking-lot behind the Monequois Professional Building the three of them had spread out like competitors in a scavenger hunt, first inside the building itself and then around the area in back.

And now it was Devers who'd found it, after fifteen minutes of searching, stuffed into a large metal garbage bin against the rear wall, with papers strewn over it to keep it from casual eyes.

Webb had been going through the pile of leaves at the far corner of the lot, Parker had been searching the hedge along the rear boundary line of the property. They both trotted over to find Devers grinning in the light from the Buick, an old canvas suitcase sitting on top of the now-closed garbage bin.

Webb said, "Is that it?"

"We'll see," Parker said. "Open it."

"Right," said Devers.

It wasn't locked. Devers flipped open the two catches, raised the lid, and they were looking at a jumbled untidy mass of bills.

Parker said, "Good. Put it in the car, switch the lights off, come up to the office." He turned to Webb. "Come on with me."

"Right."

The back door wouldn't close properly since they'd gone through it the last time. Parker led the way into the building and up the stairs, Webb following him, saying as they started down the hall toward Godden's office, "What do we want up here?"

"The body."

"If he's dead."

"He'll be dead," Parker said.

They'd left the office as they'd found it, light on and door ajar, and when they went in now nothing had changed. Ralph was lying with his face turned so he was staring under the desk. Parker went on one knee beside him, closed his hand against Ralph's throat.

Webb, leaning over the desk, said, "Alive or dead?"

Parker didn't answer for a moment. His arm showed strain. Then he took his hand away and said, "Dead. We need something to roll him in, so we don't trail blood."

"Rug in the other office."

"Good. Take his feet."

They carried the body to the outer office, put it on the small rug in front of the receptionist's desk. When they rolled the rug, Ralph's feet protruded from the knees down.

Parker said, "We want the money cases, too."

They went back to the inner office, got the two money cases, carried them out to the hall. Then Parker went back to the office to look things over. There were stains on the carpet behind the desk, but there was nothing to be done about that. No other signs out of the ordinary, and the stains could only be seen if you went around behind the desk. Parker switched off the light, went to the outer office, and he and Webb carried the body out to the hall. They shut the door so it locked, and Devers arrived saying, "What's up?"

Webb told him, "We're transporting a stiff."

Parker said, "Can you carry those two cases? Don't make a lot of marks on the walls."

"I'll do my best."

Parker and Webb picked up the body again and carried

it out to the car. Devers followed, carrying the cases one at a time, bringing one partway and going back for the other and carrying that farther and going back for the first and so on. Because Parker and Webb moved more slowly, Devers could keep up with them and even run ahead and open the tailgate of the Buick for them.

The back of the Buick was crowded with the suitcase, metal cases and body. Parker and the other two climbed in the front and Webb said, "Where now?"

"Godden's house."

6

THE DOCTOR was sitting on the floor where they'd left him, still tied and gagged. Webb went directly to the dresser when Parker turned on the light, picked up Godden's keys, and went out to switch cars, putting Godden's car in the drive and the Buick in the garage.

Parker sat on the bed. "Listen close," he said. "Because of you, things got screwed up. We can't use our hideout now, we'd never get out there any more, it's almost light already. Three of my friends are dead, and two thirds of the money is gone. If I didn't have any use for you I'd kill you now with a wire hanger. But I can use you, so you've got a shot at living. Cooperate and you'll be all right. Screw up again and it's all over."

Godden nodded vigorously.

"All right." Parker went over and removed the gag. "Don't do a lot of talking," he said. "Just answer the questions I ask you."

Godden nodded again. "I will." His voice sounded rusty, there were red marks on his cheeks where the gag had bit. The blood on his forehead had dried, so no more was seeping out.

Parker went back and sat on the edge of the bed again. He said, "How long is your wife out of town for?"

"Five more days. She'll be back Monday afternoon. That is, the two of us are supposed to be back Monday afternoon."

"You were leaving?"

"Friday. Friday afternoon."

"Were you due in your office today?"

"You mean tomorrow? The day that's starting?"
"It's twenty after four in the morning. I mean today."
"Yes, of course."
"How many patients today?"
"Four. Well, three, not counting Ralph Hochberg."
"Roger St Cloud?"
"Yes. Is he—?"
"That's two," Parker said. "What time's the first session?"
"Ten o'clock. But that would have been Ralph. The next one would be at eleven."
"In the morning," Parker said, "call those two patients, tell them you won't be in today."
Godden nodded. "All right."
"But wait till after the law talks to you."
Godden looked surprised. "The law? You mean the police?"
"Your boy Roger barricaded himself in the house and shot it out with the cops."
"My God!"
"They'll be calling you. If you hear about it some other legitimate way first, you call them, offer full cooperation. Offer to talk to them, tell them anything they want to know. But you don't want to go to them, you want them to come to you."
"What if they insist?"
"You insist."
"But, won't they be suspicious?"
"No," Parker said. "When they come here, give them the whole rundown on Roger, anything you want to say. But you keep cool about us."
"You'll be here? This is where you're going to hide out?"
"If you tip about us," Parker said, "the least you'll get is your connection with the air base heist found out by the law. The worst you'll get is a bullet in the head."
"If I come out of this with my skin," Godden said, "I'll consider myself well ahead. Ellen Fusco told me about you, Parker, but I underestimated you, I didn't really listen to what she was saying." His face clouded. "I underestimated

Roger, too."

"Just keep remembering that," Parker said. He got to his feet. "See you in the morning."

"You're going to leave me here like this?"

Parker went out, switching off the light.

There was a small light on in the kitchen now, enough to allow him to make his way around in the house. He went down to the kitchen and found Webb at the refrigerator. Webb looked around, a container of milk in one hand and a piece of pound cake in the other. "I was starved."

"Where's Devers?"

"Here," Devers said, coming in grinning, lugging the suitcase. "I thought we could divvy up before I went back."

Parker looked at him. "Back where?"

Devers was blank. "Back to Ellen's place, where else?"

Parker said, "Some time tomorrow the law's going to find those three bodies up by the lodge. Either tomorrow or the next day they'll get a fingerprint report, and one of those bodies is going to belong to a guy named Martin Fusco. They're going to look around, and they're going to see an ex-wife of Martin Fusco's living right here in town. Coincidence. They'll go talk to the ex-wife, and they'll find out she's shacked up with a guy from the finance office out at the air base. Coincidence number two."

Devers was pale. "Christ on a crutch. How do I get out of it? I just keep saying no. What can they do? I keep saying no, it's a coincidence, what can they do about it?"

Webb, his mouth full of pound cake, said, "They'll lean on you, buddy. They'll lean hard."

"I can hold out."

Parker said, "Can Ellen? They'll lean on her, too."

"I'd say kill her," Webb said thoughtfully, "but then they'd lean on you harder. And then if they get you they've got you on murder one."

Devers was looking from one to the other. "What do I do?"

"You take your forty thousand," Parker said, "and you go away."

"But I've got to finish out my enlistment!"

Parker shook his head. "Not now. Between the woman and him upstairs, they've screwed you."

"Only if they get Fusco's body," Devers said.

Webb said, "Forget it. You're pretty safe to drive around in town, but you go out on the road now they'll be all over you. You can't even get to the lodge without going by the base."

"So they stop me. I'm clean."

"Finance office clerk. Driving around four o'clock in the morning. No destination."

Parker added, "If they pick you up on the way back, you won't be clean. Not with Fusco in the car."

Devers was getting frantic. "God damn it, there's got to be *some* way! What the hell am I going to do?"

"You're going to find the registration to Godden's car," Parker told him. "In case you get stopped. Then you're going to take his car and go over to the house and get Ellen and the kid. If she doesn't want to come with you, you'll kill her."

"I can't—"

"Then call us and tell us you can't and give us a shot at making a run for it."

Devers looked from Parker to Webb to Parker. "All right," he said. "I get her. Then what?"

"You bring her here. If the law finds her, she'll tell them about Godden, and we need Godden clean so we can hole up here. So she has to come here, too."

"How long do we hole up here?"

"Two or three days. Till the first heat lets up."

Devers made an angry bitter gesture. "Then what do I do?"

"Pick a new name for yourself, buddy," Webb told him. "And keep your head down. And hope for the best."

"You mean be on the run the rest of my life."

Webb grinned, "Like in the movies? Sleeping in hay-lofts, riding in freight cars, that what you mean?" He shook his head. "I been wanted under my own name for fifteen years. Parker here, he's wanted under more names than he can remember. We both been on the run, we're always on the run. It's a nice easy run if you know how to take it."

Devers looked at Parker. He was seeing things a new way. "You were in Puerto Rico," he said.

Webb spread his hands. "There, you see? On the run, at the Hilton hotel."

7

WHEN THE two plainclothesmen left, Parker came out of the kitchen and made a show of putting his revolver away. "That was nice," he said.

Godden was sweating, the adhesive bandage on his forehead making a dull tan patch against the gleaming pale skin. "I wouldn't want to go through that twice," he said. "Not for a million dollars."

Webb and Devers came in from the other side. "You did it for a hundred G," Webb said, "and you don't even get that."

Devers didn't say anything. He was resigned now to the impossibility of his going back, but he hated Godden for having caused it. He stood there and glared at Godden, his fists clenched at his sides.

Godden nervously touched his bandage. Do you think they believed me about this?"

"They believed everything," Parker told him. "You did good."

The story Parker had given him to tell tied together neatly enough, being grounded sufficiently in truth. When the phone had rung at ten minutes to seven this morning it was Parker who'd answered it, saying he was Godden. It was a reporter on the line, representing one of the wire services and phoning from Syracuse. Parker, being Godden, told him the news about the Roger St Cloud affair was a complete surprise to him, and of course he wouldn't be able to make a statement until he'd talked to the police.

Then Parker had roused Godden and had him phone the

police and say he'd just been called by a reporter saying Roger St Cloud had run amok. When the man at the other end substantiated the story, Godden volunteered to tell what he could about St Cloud's motives and state of mind, explaining he'd prefer the police to come to him because he'd fallen in getting out of bed to answer the reporter's call, he'd cut his head, and he didn't yet know how serious it was. Also, this news about a patient of his had shaken him badly.

The cop was sympathetic, and said a couple of men would be around sometime in the morning. They'd arrived at ten-fifteen, two plainclothesmen who already knew about the head injury, who were polite and deferential, and who obviously didn't suspect Dr Fred Godden of anything. But why should they?

Now it was quarter to eleven, and in the half-hour they'd been here the two cops had shown nothing but interest in Godden's monologue on Roger St Cloud. Godden had been nervous at first, but the police would have other explanations for that, and when he'd warmed into his description of Roger the nervousness vanished. He was, after all, engaging in shoptalk.

The plainclothesmen hadn't said anything about Roger being involved in last night's robbery at the air base, but the two events had been linked in the radio news since the nine o'clock broadcast. Nor had the radio said anything about the bodies up at the lodge yet, but the nine-thirty news had reported the finding of the bus. "Some of the bandits may have crossed the border into Canada under cover of darkness."

They should be safe now, at least for a while. Godden had already called those of his patients he was to have seen that day and the next, telling them that under the circumstances naturally he wouldn't be in the office till next week. After a few more reporters had called — the criminal's analyst having replaced the criminal's clergyman as a source of sidelight stories — there was nothing unusual in Godden leaving his phone off the hook.

The last item was Godden's wife. Parker said, "Call your

wife now. She'll want to come back here, but tell her no. Tell her you'll be coming along Friday as planned, unless the police want to talk to you again, and if they do you'll be there Saturday. Tell her not to try calling you back because reporters have been bothering you and you aren't answering the phone."

"All right," Godden said. He made the call, did more listening than talking, and finally got across all of the message that Parker wanted. When he hung up he looked uncertainly at Parker and said, "There's another call I should make."

"Who?"

"There's a young lady. I would have seen her tonight."

"Here?"

"No, her place."

"Call her. Devers, get on the kitchen extension. If the woman doesn't sound right, let me know."

"Right." Devers went out to the kitchen on the double, and it was clear he hoped Godden was trying something cute.

But Godden wasn't. He called his young lady, explained that the Roger St Cloud business had loused everything up, and promised to see her next week, Tuesday or Wednesday at the latest.

When he was done with that call, and Devers had come back into the living-room to give a disgusted shake of the head, Parker said, "All right. Back to your room."

Godden got to his feet, trying a smile. "You don't have to tie me up again, you know," he said. "You can trust me. I want to get clear of this mess just as much as you do."

"You bastard," Devers said.

Godden turned to him, spreading his hands. "I'm sorry for what's happened to you, believe me I am. I didn't want any of this. I didn't want anybody dead, anybody ruined. The worst I wanted was to take your money away."

"You rotten bastard," Devers said.

Parker said, "That's all. Godden, go upstairs. Webb, take him. Devers, take a look at your woman."

Devers grimaced. "My woman," he said in disgust, and turned away, and walked out of the room.

Ellen and her baby were being kept in the room once occupied by Godden's children. According to Devers, she hadn't wanted to come with him at first when he'd gone for her last night, she'd been sure she could bluff it out with the police. But when he'd assured her it was all up for them all, that being the ex-wife of one of the heistmen and at the same time shacked up with a finance office clerk from the air base left her in no position to try a bluff with the law, and that her choice was between coming with him or being silenced for ever as dangerous to the ones who were left, she'd reluctantly seen the light. Then she'd wanted to do a lot of packing, but Devers had cut that short, and she'd arrived with her daughter and one hastily stuffed overnight case.

When Devers had brought her in she was being so erratic, fluctuating so badly among panic and guilt and despair and indignation, that Parker decided she was untrustworthy, and she'd been kept under lock and key ever since. Parker had guaranteed her silence during the plainclothesmen's visit just now by letting her know her daughter would pay as much as she would for any trouble she caused. Any more trouble.

Now Parker went out to the kitchen and turned on the radio to hear the eleven o'clock news. They had a breathing spell now, shaky and complicated but with a chance of working out. Ralph Hochberg's body was with the two money cases under a tarp in the basement. The money was still in the suitcase over by the refrigerator. Godden was a prisoner in one room, Ellen and her kid were prisoners in another, and no one else was left for the law to talk to and learn anything troublesome. They were covered against visitors and callers on the telephone. With luck, they'd be able to stay here another two days, until Saturday. With luck, another two days was all they'd need.

When Webb and Devers came into the kitchen, both to say their charges were under control, Parker said, "Let's have that suitcase. Time to see how much we've got left."

They sat around the kitchen table with the suitcase open in front of them and started counting. When they were done it came to a total of one hundred twenty-six thousand, five hundred eighty-three dollars. Parker did some figuring with pencil and paper and said, "That's forty-two thousand, one hundred ninety-four for each of us, with a dollar left over."

Webb rooted through the pile of money on the table found a single, crumpled it and threw it on the floor. "Now it's even," he said.

Devers began to laugh. When it seemed as though the laughter was getting hysterical Parker said, "Stop it." Devers stopped, looked at Parker, and got up from the table and went into the living-room.

Webb said, "What about him?"

"We'll wait and see."

They kept the radio on. The one o'clock news led off with the discovery of the bodies at the lodge, though with no identification of any of them, and followed with an *authorities-are-looking-for* on Devers and Ellen Fusco. No accusations, no statement that either of them was believed to be part of the mob. Just that they were being sought for questioning. The descriptions the newscaster gave fit Devers and Ellen, but they also fit a million or so other people in the world.

Webb said, "They must of found the lodge this morning. They were keeping it quiet until they were sure Devers wasn't coming home."

After a while Devers came in from the living-room. He'd found Godden's liquor cabinet, and had a glass of warm Scotch in his hand. "You ought to come in and watch television," he said. "They got my picture on televison."

Webb looked up at him. "Is that right? You're a celebrity."

"I'm a celebrity." Devers was a little drunk already, just enough to dull all his responses.

Webb said, "A celebrity oughta have ice. Lemme bring you in some ice."

Devers stood in the middle of the kitchen floor while Webb found an ice bucket and emptied two trays of cubes into it. Devers had the frown of the morose drunk on his face, the look of a man who suspects someone is pulling a huge complicated unfathomable practical joke on him.

Webb grabbed up the ice bucket and said, "Come on,

Stan, I'll drink you under the table." He led Devers back to the living-room.

Later on Parker let Ellen out to make dinner. She too was dulled in her reactions now, docile but sullen. Pam, her little girl, knowing something was wrong, stuck close to her mother's knee all the time, looking round-eyed out at the world.

They all had dinner together, with the exception of Godden, who afterwards got a tray in his room. Parker felt there were too many people at the table who hated Godden, there was no point looking for trouble.

Devers wasn't sobered much by dinner. Afterwards, while Ellen went back to her room and Parker went into the living-room to watch television, Devers and Webb took over the kitchen. Devers told sex stories, Webb told crime stories. They both laughed a lot. Parker stayed sober, watched television, watched on the eleven o'clock news films of the lodge and of the ambulance bringing the bodies down the dirt road. Ellen Fusco's mother appeared on the screen, asking her daughter to come back, to at least let Pamela come to live with her grandma. There were photos of Devers and Ellen.

Devers passed out around two in the morning, and Webb went to Parker, weaving a little, and said, "He'll be all right. He'll be okay, Parker. He's just got to get used to it."

"I thought he'd work out," Parker said.

Friday was slow and dull. People came to the door a few times, but always gave up after a while. Devers had a hangover and spent most of the day in the kitchen trying different cures. Webb found a deck of cards and played game after game of solitaire. Ellen was calmer now, and more sensible, and realized she had no place else to go, so she and her daughter had the run of the house. Godden was still being tied up and kept in his room. Parker prowled around watching and waiting.

Friday night, Devers and Webb got drunk again, played gin rummy, told the same stories they'd told the night before. Ellen put her daughter to bed and came to Parker and said, "Stan isn't going to want me to go with him now. I don't blame him. But I don't have any money, any place to go."

Parker looked at her. "What do you want?"

"A little money. Not a lot."

"Maybe Devers will give you a piece of his cut. Ask him."

"I don't have any place to go," she said, and panic began to play again behind her eyes.

Parker didn't want her going back to being frantic and erratic. To keep her calm, he said, "I'll talk it over with Webb. We'll work something out for you by tomorrow."

"Thank you," she said tonelessly, and walked away.

Devers passed out about one o'clock that night, and Webb came into the living-room to finish his drinking with Parker. "Great kid," he said. "He'll stay in this line, won't he?"

"Probably," Parker said.

Webb finished his drink, put the glass on the floor beside his chair. "When do you figure we can get out of here?"

"Maybe tomorrow night. They're not really looking around here any more."

"They figure we're in Alaska by now."

Parker didn't say anything, and when he looked over toward Webb a minute later he was asleep.

The only light in the house now came from the television set. Parker sat in front of it, looking at it, not really paying attention to it, and when the sermon ended and the national anthem ended and the screen went to snow he didn't bother turning it off. A while later, still facing the empty screen he went to sleep.

8

PARKER WOKE up when Webb touched his arm. Cartoons were jumping on the television screen. Gray light touched the drapes covering the picture window. Parker looked at his watch and the time was seven-forty.

Webb looked serious. Keeping his voice low, he said, "Better come take a look."

Parker went with him, up to Godden's room. Godden, his arms and legs still tied, was lying on his side on the bed, his throat cut. The sheet was soaked with his blood.

Parker said, "The woman."

"Gone. Left this."

The note was scrawled hastily with pencil on brown wrapping-paper, the letters large and ragged. It said:

I won't say where you are. I have to bring Pam to my mother. I'm sorry.

Webb said, "What now?"

Parker shook his head. "I wish I knew when she left."

"I heard the door close, that's what woke me. Less than five minutes."

"Then we get out of here," Parker said.

They went down to the kitchen and woke Devers and showed him the note and told him about Godden. Parker said, "Be sober, boy. We've got to get out of here now."

"Why? You think she'll talk?"

"She won't have to talk. A crazy woman staggering around a little town like this, seven-thirty in the morning, how far do you think she'll get? Six blocks? Ten blocks? Then they pick her up, they say maybe the others are in the same neighborhood. Somebody says, that head doctor's in that neighborhood. Somebody says, take a look over there, Joe."

Devers was sober. He said, "How much time have we got?"

"Until they get organized. Until somebody notices it's Godden's neighborhood. Maybe an hour, maybe less."

"Christ." Devers went over to the kitchen sink, ran cold water, splashed it on his face, dried with a dish towel. "Where do we go?" he said.

"You ride with me for a while," Parker told him.

They got their gear and went out to the cars. Parker and Devers took Godden's dark green Cadillac. Parker's suitcase, with his gear and his part of the money, and a small case of Godden's that Devers had taken to carry his cut, went into the trunk. Parker drove.

They were in West Monequois, and the best direction to go was away, so they headed out to Route 11 and traveled west toward Potsdam. Webb's Buick stayed behind them a while, but he turned south at Moria. Parker went on to Lawrenceville, switched to an unnumbered back road down through Buckton and Southville, and picked up 56 at Colton. He headed south.

They kept the car radio on. The robbery news was already becoming stale, being now into its third day with nothing sensational happening for the last two. No mention of Ellen Fusco yet.

Devers said, "This car's going to get hot soon. Once they get to Godden's house."

"I know it."

"What's our chances?"

"We need a city," Parker said. "You can disappear in a city. There's nothing up here but mountains."

There was a New York State roadmap in the glove compartment. Devers studied it and finally said, "Our best bet's Albany."

"How far?"

"Where are we?"

"Coming into something called Sevey," Parker told him.

Devers studied the map. "About a hundred and sixty. Some of it's good road." He gave a bitter grin. "Same road I took you up on," he said.

9

IT MADE the eleven o'clock news, just as they were passing Glen Falls on the Northway, about fifty miles from Albany. "Mrs Ellen Fusco, sought in connection with Wednesday night's payroll robbery at Monequois Air Force Base in upstate New York, walked into the home of her parents, Mr and Mrs Herbert Atkinson of Monequois, early this morning, her three-year-old daughter Pamela in her arms. Dazed, distraught, unable to tell police her whereabouts the last three days—"

"Good," Devers said. He looked over at Parker. "She's making up for it," he said.

"If they let the news out," Parker said, "it's because they've already traced her back to the Godden house. Time to ditch this car. What's the next exit off this thing?"

Devers looked at the map. "Saratoga."

"We'll unload it there."

Parker kept it at the legal maximum the ten miles to the Saratoga exit, one eye always on the rear-view mirror. Saturday traffic was building up, and a green Cadillac wasn't that out of place, but they could only push their luck so far.

Parker left the car in downtown Saratoga, at a meter. He and Devers walked the three blocks to the bus depot and boarded the eleven-thirty express to Albany. They got to Albany at twelve-oh-five, and Parker said, "This is where we split. You need somebody to show you how things work, and I don't have the time for that now. There's a friend of mine named Handy McKay, he's retired now, runs a diner in a place called Presque Isle, in Maine. You go up there, tell him you're from me. You can give him the story. He'll take care of you."

Devers said, "Thanks. This isn't the way I had it planned, but what the hell."

"That's right," Parker said.

10

SHE WAS on her chaise longue, face up to the sun. She was wearing the suit with the black trunks and the black and white top. Her sunglasses had white rims. Towel and book and cigarettes and suntan lotion were on the sand beside her. She seemed to be asleep.

Parker had gone up to the room first and put on his trunks. He padded across the sand and sat down on the chaise beside her. "You're more tanned now than you were," he said.

Claire started. She looked at him, lifted her sunglasses and squinted at him under them. "You did come back," she said.

"I always will."

"Good. Where shall we eat tonight?"

"Mallorquina."

"Good, I like that. Shall we go to the casino afterwards?"

"Yes," he said.